Arranged

Suddenly Married
Book 3

By: Lynna Farlight

Chapter 1

The bright winter moon hung low over the fields, saying its goodbyes, as morning awakened slowly. Spring had begun to peek through, one flower at a time, but Susannah could not see the tiny blooms in the darkness as she walked swiftly through the chilly air from the barn to the house. She had awoken extremely early, as always, and soon had the oven warming and the bread rising before anyone else was up.

A torn piece of clothing, belonging to one of the younger kids, lay waiting for her in her chair in the corner. She glanced around, to be sure all tasks had been completed. She had awakened her cousins, opened the curtains, chopped a few potatoes and set out the skillet and butter. The coffee was prepared and the bread was nearly ready to bake. Susannah nodded and stepped towards her chair across the small sitting room beside the kitchen, but before her foot left the wooden floor by the dining table and landed on the large braided rug in front of the sitting room fireplace, a motion in the hall caught her attention. Someone was approaching. Susannah glanced at the window to see the beginnings of sunrise. Her aunt was the latest riser, as usual. Susannah had already sent the little ones out to their chores, and their mother could not even been bothered to awaken before them, but that was nothing new.

Aunt Jane held out her hand, waiting for the mug of ready coffee, with a splash of milk and two sugar cubes, that Susannah was required to have ready to hand her when she walked into the kitchen each morning. Susannah gave her the hot clay mug and proceeded to her chair. She picked up what turned out to be her five-year-old cousin's best dress shirt with a long rip along the left sleeve. Without a word, Susannah settled into the hardbacked wooden chair and chose a spool of white thread from the sewing basket on the floor nearby.

Aunt Jane began fiddling with the long wooden spoon that Susannah would use to scramble the eggs, as soon as the boys brought them in. Jane liked to toy with tools, as if she were ever going to used them. "Has your uncle returned from town yet?" She asked drowsily, taking a long sip of her coffee.

"Uh...no," Susannah answered, in her soft voice.

She was a little startled. Her aunt and uncle never shared much information with her about whatever might be going on with them, but she usually knew anyway, somehow, but this time she had not even realized that Uncle Byron was not on the property. He was usually out somewhere, around this time, doing some farm related task or other. He'd wander in at breakfast time, expecting it to be laid out and ready, but apparently, today, he had some errand to run. Susannah wasn't sure what could take him to town before sunrise, but she suspected it had something to do with the loan being due on the farm and the fact that they could not repay it.

Jane usually meandered over to her pillowed chair by the fire around this time, to drink her coffee in peace, with her feet on her tiny footstool. She'd talk the whole time Susannah cooked, issuing commands and instructions for the day and complaining and commenting on all of Susannah's efforts, past, present and future. Quiet Susannah would fry potatoes, while the bread baked, praise the little boys when they brought in the milk and eggs and then proceed to scramble up breakfast while saying "Yes, ma'am" and "No, ma'am" to her aunt's ramblings. It had been her routine for ten years, and Susannah could hardly imagine any other kind of morning, but today, Aunt Jane did not settle into the cushiest chair in the room and set her mouth to jammering, instead she sat down at the table and stared anxiously out the window in silence, while Susannah nervously sewed, wondering what was going on.

A moment later they heard the jangle of hitching gear as the wagon rolled in and Uncle Byron entered the house, without putting the horses away. Aunt Jane stared at him, for once at a loss for words. He stared back at her for a moment, before sitting down at the empty table. Neither of them looked at Susannah or acknowledged her presence. Something very serious was happening. She could feel it in the air.

While the silence still hung heavy in the room, Susannah caught a glimpse of young Marigold coming down the hall. It was the ten-year-old's usual time to set the table. With a quick movement of her hand and a commanding look in her eye, Susannah waved the child away. Startled, Marigold turned and disappeared, returning to the back porch where she had been folding laundry pulled from the line last night. Susannah's head turned back to her aunt and uncle as Aunt Jane finally spoke.

"Well?!" she demanded, "Stop keeping me in suspense and just spit it out! Did you fix the problem or not?"

Byron bristled at her tone, his eyebrows settling into an angry line. "It's fine now. It's all been arranged."

"Arranged?" Aunt Jane looked perplexed. "What's been arranged?"

Susannah could not sew. Her hands had long settled into her lap. Her eyes bobbed back and forth from her uncle's mouth to her aunt's as she followed the conversation.

"Well, as you know, Mr. Bridges does not make exceptions when it comes to defaulting on a loan….He…he never ever has… before….." Byron let his words drag out, the anger slipping from his eyes. He tilted his head a little and stared down at his hands on the rough-hewn tabletop.

"But…b-but he made an exception this time?" Jane begged. "Please say that he did. Oh, what are we going to do?" She suddenly clasped her hands together and began wringing them like some desperate heroine from a tragic dime novel.

"Oh, calm down!" Byron said sharply, hating his wife's constant drama. "I told you, we made an arrangement. I'm just trying to make you understand that he would only make an exception in return for something...well....significant." He did not meet his wife's eyes.

Jane's expression grew cold and her hands stopped moving. "What did you do, Byron Kelly!"

"I saved this farm! That's what I did!" Byron snapped, jumping up from his chair and knocking it over in the process.

Jane rose regally from her chair with slow movements and folded her arms across her chest. "What did you promise the banker, Byron?" she growled, squinting her eyes in angry suspicion.

Byron took a deep breath and drew himself up to his fullest height, then spoke clearly. "He will allow us to continue to make payments as we have been, for as long as it takes to pay off the loan, in exchange for... Elsie...marrying his son....today."

Jane blinked. Her mouth dropped open. After a few seconds of pure shock, she blurted, "I beg your pardon?"

"You heard me." Byron held his ground, glaring at his wife.

Jane slowly sat back in her chair, as if she needed the support. She looked down at the table and said softly, "Surely, you're just jesting with me, Byron. Elsie is betrothed to Josh. The wedding is in a month!" Her voice rose a little and her head popped up to face her husband.

"Joshua Woods is a fine young man," Byron acknowledged, his tone calming. "But sacrifices must be made sometimes." He picked up his chair and sat down in it again. A few quiet breaths passed. Susannah could not believe what she was hearing.

Finally, Jane gulped air and asked, "And just why does Jeffrey

Bridges need a wife so…so suddenly? And why can't he find one on his own?"

"Well, he doesn't want one. It's a long story," Byron said, leaning back in his chair as if he were feeling abruptly tired. "Something about going west, and an argument with his mother, and an agreement with his father about a loan for his start-up costs. It's all very rushed and well, no one seems to be very happy. It looks like Mr. Bridges is forcing his son into this because of his wife. That man never could say no to her."

"Unlike some people I know," Jane muttered. "I begged you not to invest in those ridiculous foreign beans that nobody bought and to not spend our money on that stupid horse of yours, but no, you don't do nothin' the way I want. Never have. Why, I could beg you till I was blue in the face not to do this to Elsie, but no, you don't care one lick about how I feel."

"You always find a way to make everything about you!" Byron's fist hit the table. "You got some plan for where we'd go with all these younguns if we lose our land? Hmmm? You just tell me, if you know so much?"

The two people glared at each other, locked in a familiar pattern of stubbornness, their chests heaving up and down. Finally, Byron leaned back again. "It's the only way. It's this or we lose everything. It's Elsie's duty to obey me, and to do what she can for her family. I'm sure she'll be glad to do this for us.

"Oh, you're sure are you?" Jane retorted. "She loves that boy, you know. Something neither of us would know anything about."

"Well, then, we certainly know it ain't necessary for marriage," Byron said, in a clipped tone filled with obstinace. "Ain't never had hide nor hair of it in ours and we're still here."

Jane gasped at the painful insult, even though she had brought up the idea first.

Byron and Jane Kelly often seemed to think that their niece was a piece of the furniture. When they had arguments with

Susannah nearby, it was as if she just blended into the wall, as far they were concerned. This was possible partly because of Susannah's quiet temperament, but mostly because she meant very little to them. No one meant much to them except themselves. Even their own kids received only occasional bursts of mild affection, such as Jane's brief protest against ripping away Elsie's cherished future, a protest which was immediately turned into somehow being centered on Jane. Susannah had long since given up on being hurt or angry by her aunt's and uncle's lack of caring for her, or anyone. It was simply their nature. As she had grown and matured, Susannah even began to pity her older relatives for their inability to feel the best things in life, like love or gratitude. This morning they were exhibiting their customary indifference to Susannah's presence as they carried on their very personal discussion in front of her, barely noticing that she was even there. That's why they practically jumped out of their skins when Susannah spoke and startled Byron and Jane into a moment of speechlessness.

"I'll do it," she said, softly, but clearly.

Flinching, the two heads swiveled towards her.

Her aunt and uncle had always treated her as little more than a servant, and she had no great affection for them, just as they didn't for her, but Elsie was the dearest person in the world to Susannah. Sweet kind Elsie, who brought a smile to everyone's face when she entered a room. She couldn't let this happen to her, not when Elsie had loved quiet Joshua Woods since they were little. It was a tragedy to take that away from them.

Susannah felt her hands lower into her lap and settle on top of the torn shirt she'd been working on. For a second, the hands had been headed to cover her mouth in shock at what she had said, but she caught them midway. Yes, she was surprised by the words that had tumbled out of her mouth, but yes, she was also certain of them as well. She felt her own suppressed dreams bubbling up inside her and she opened her mouth to do something very out of character, she repeated herself and she did it in a strong voice. "I'll do it, Uncle Byron. I'll do it."

Byron had recovered his composure. "Why are you interrupting our conversation? Explain yourself."

"Well,…um….," Susannah slowly rose to face her uncle, "I'd…um…I'd like to help." She cleared her throat, trying to think of the best words that would get through to her uncle. He did not care that this was the opportunity she had been waiting for for years. He did not care that she wanted out of this life or dreamed of a new one. She must explain in terms he *did* care about. "There's no need to break Elsie's engagement and have Josh's family upset with our family." To say nothing of breaking the hearts of the two young people. That wouldn't mean anything to Byron, but damaging his standing in town, his relationships with other families, that mattered to him. "Afterall," Susannah continued, "It sounds to me like neither Jeffrey nor his father would care which one of us girls gets married today, as long as Mrs. Bridges gets her son married off like she wants. Surely, it won't matter if it's me instead of Elsie."

Byron's eyes were widening as he considered this new prospect. Susannah and Jane could almost see wheels turning in his head.

"Now, wait just a minute!" Jane stood up just so she could stomp her foot indignantly. "Don't tell me you're considering this! Susannah can't leave! Who will do all her work? I need her to help me." The last part came out close to a child's whine.

"No, no, no." Byron rose grinning. "This could work. Afterall, it's my duty to see that my brother's daughter gets herself married off. I hadn't given it much thought before, but it really is my duty, I think. Don't you agree?" He didn't even look at his wife as he said it.

"No! I don't agree! No!" Jane said, leaning towards Byron, but he ignored her.

"Come now, it's a better match. Sue won't be pinin' after another boy, like Elsie would, plus, Sue and Jeff are closer in age." He finally looked at Susannah. "What are you now, about eighteen?"

"Twenty," Susannah corrected, but Byron was barely listening. Her birthday had come and gone two days ago, but no one had noticed.

"See? I should have taken care of this long ago. Why, this is far better than upsetting our Elsie or the Woods family." He stepped towards the door. "You just hurry along now, Sue, and get your things. We'll leave after breakfast."

Susannah's stomach was doing summersaults. Was this really happening? She stumbled towards the door.

"But she hasn't even *made* breakfast yet! Byron, you can't do this to me!" Jane's face was red and angry tears welled in her eyes.

"Oh, hush, Jane. You'll be doing that yourself from now on. So, you best get started." He opened the door and Susannah rushed out as her uncle said sarcastically to his wife, "You *can* make eggs, can't you dear?" Then the door slammed behind her.

***

Five-year-old Seth, six-year-old Teddy and twelve-year-old Jessica were surprised to see their cousin, Susannah, walking away from the house before breakfast, her steps growing faster with every yard covered. She told them that all was well and they must get their basket of eggs and buckets of milk inside. They went in the house, perplexed at this unprecedented disturbance in their morning routine, and Susannah headed into the barn.

The sun was high enough to see now, and she gathered her few things by its light, shining through the loft window. She started by wrapping her father's tiny Bible, carefully, in her only pair of knit stockings. As she was folding her overmended nightgown, followed by an equally overmended hand-me-down cloak, she turned at a sound, to see Elsie climbing the ladder into the loft.

"Susannah! What on earth?!" Susannah flashed her cousin a quick smile, before the sixteen-year-old continued. "There I am just churning away at the butter. I've got yesterday's milk tins empty all around me, like any other morning, just watching the sun rise, when Marigold comes back to the porch saying you sent her out and something was going on." She put her hands on her hips. "We cracked the door a little to listen and….and..Susie, I..I don't even know where to start! Is it true? Did I hear it right?"

"If you heard that I'm off to marry Jeffrey Bridges this morning, then you heard right," Susannah said softly, dropping a faded handkerchief her mother had given her into her aging carpet bag. It was the same bag she had brought with her ten years ago, when she first arrived on her uncle's farm.

Walking with a slow stunned cadence, Elsie found her way to Susannah's small bed and sat down, as if her legs would not hold her. She stared into space. "I…I can't believe it. It's so…so…"

"Sudden?" Susannah finished for her. "I know, but it's my chance and I'm jumping at it."

After a few more breaths, the news seemed to have sunk in. Elsie opened her mouth and her voice was calmer. "Are you really sure, Susannah? Really sure? Ma's fit to be tied!"

"I know and I'm sorry for that, but I….," Susannah stopped rolling up her second dress and turned to look at her cousin. Her thoughts rolled around and around like the worn cloth in her hands. She hesitated, trying to grasp her reasoning. "She might never let me, otherwise. I have to do this now, while I can. I… I want to go…just…go. You know that." She returned to her work.

"Of course, I do," Elsie replied. "Do you think I don't notice things? I know that when Ma took you out of school when you were thirteen, it wasn't because she needed help around the house, it was because she didn't want any boys drawn to that beautiful dark red hair or the beautiful personality beneath it."

Susannah blushed a little, reaching for her comb and other small items that lay on the windowsill. "Oh, hush now, Elsie."

"No, I won't hush, not this time. I saw the way she always

ordered you to head to the wagon just before the sermon was over each Sunday, so no boys could ever talk to you. Ma wants you to stay her drudge forever and for you to never find a way out. Everybody knows it."

"You shouldn't speak so about your Ma. It's disrespectful." Susannah looked right at her cousin. This was not like her. Rarely did anything unkind come out of her mouth.

"It's the truth, stated plainly," Elsie defended herself.

She reached out to hold Susannah's hand, pulling her down to sit on the bed beside her. They glanced around for a moment at the tiny space, surrounded by mounds of hay. A few pegs on the wall, a windowsill for a shelf and this meager hay-filled mattress propped on a row of chopped logs, to raise it a little, was all the Kellys had given their niece in return for her patient hard work since childhood. Elsie fingered the single threadbare quilt beneath them.

"I know your dreams, Susie," she whispered. "The little kitchen and garden you've always wanted. I haven't forgotten the times you've confided in me how much you want to see some other place outside of this town and get out from under Ma's thumb and be free, but are you really sure about this? It's so out of the blue. How can you possibly have put enough thought into it?"

"Sometimes we don't have that luxury," Susannah answered, "And, in a way, I've been thinking about it for years. This could be my one and only opportunity and I'll not let it slip by. I've never really spoken to Jeffrey, but he seems like a good enough fellow. I'll be fine, as long as he builds us a little house and lets me piddle in my kitchen and garden and they'll be my very own. That's all I've ever wanted. Besides, there's no other way. Do you want to lose the farm or…." The young woman left the sentence unfinished because she did not want her cousin to dwell on the fact that Susannah was doing this for her, so she could marry her sweetheart, but Elsie knew. The two girls let the words hang in the air for a moment, then Elsie sighed, resigned.

"Well, then I wish you happiness and I thank you with all my heart for saving me from…from losing Josh." She sighed again, looking down at her lap, sadly. "At least, you chose this. I can't believe I was almost forced to be traded like chattel to some other boy in exchange for an extension on a loan. How could Pa do that to me? How could any father even think of such a thing? But why am I surprised? He doesn't care about me."

Susannah held Elsie's shoulders until she looked up. "We've talked about this. There is no point in such thinking. In one month, you will leave your Pa behind and begin your own life. Don't burden your heart with dark uncharitable thoughts."

Elsie sighed again. "You're right and I'm sorry I made this about me for a second there. I don't want Ma to rub off on me in that way."

"You could never be like your mother," Susannah stated matter-of-factly, standing and glancing around the small space, but she had so few belongings, there was no way she could have forgotten anything, "And you're right, I have chosen this, and I'm excited about it, so you don't need to thank me. I'm the one who is grateful to finally be getting what I want, for the first time since I was a little girl."

Elsie stood as well, brushing off her skirt. "Well, let's get going then. This next part might be hard, but I'll help you through it. I won't let Ma talk Pa out of this. I'm so happy you're getting out, Susannah. I was so worried about leaving you here next month. Now, we can both be off to new lives."

"Yes," Susannah answered, putting her arm through her carpet-bag handle and starting down the ladder, "And we must write to each other, as often as possible. I know where you'll be, and I'll send you a letter telling you where I am, as soon as I get the chance."

Chapter 2

All through a half-burnt breakfast, Jane glared at Susannah in dead silence and refused to eat. She pressed her lips together and pouted like a child, but Susannah did not acknowledge her. She preferred to spend the time mentally saying goodbye to this place she had lived for ten years. She hesitated to call it 'home' even in her thoughts. It had never felt like a true home to Susannah. She looked around at the kitchen where she had cooked a thousand meals and the hardbacked chair in the tiny sitting room where she had sewed until her fingers could not hold the needle anymore. She stared out the window at the fields where she had occasionally taken a walk, while her aunt napped or visited friends, but mostly she looked at her young cousins. She drank in their faces and tried to plan all the things she would say to them when it was time to leave them behind.

Finally, the family drove the hour and a half to Seagleton, the only town Susannah had seen since her arrival at the age of ten, and the only town any of the children had ever known. Jane sat up front with her arms crossed angrily over her chest the whole time, but Susannah sat in the back with her cousins, telling them, softly, all the many things she wanted to tell them. She encouraged each one to pursue their strengths, take care of each other and be obedient and respectful as they grew up. She told them she loved them to pieces and promised to write to each of them as often as she could. Then she let them cheer themselves up with their own make-believe stories of all the adventures she might be about to embark upon out in the great unknown.

When they arrived at the church, Elsie took Susannah into the foyer, while Jane and Byron ushered the rest of the children into the pews.

"Oh, we should have done something about your...your...um... outfit," Elsie mumbled, smoothing down Susannah's shabby patched dress. She had been wearing it for five years and she only had one other.

Susannah smiled. "Done something," she chuckled softly. "What could we have done with this?" She gestured at a fraying spot on her cuff before tucking the loose threads inside against her wrist. "Don't worry about it. This is not a typical wedding and you know things like clothes don't matter that much to me."

"Only because Ma never let you have nice things, so you learned not to care. Oh, Susie, I do hope this new life leads to better things. Nice clothes, your own home....and....that you'll be treated better."

"I was always treated just fine by you, Elsie, and the children. That was enough for me." She squeezed her cousin's arm. "Don't fret so."

"Well, pinch your cheeks, and let's at least make your hair look nice. All those russet waves can make any ensemble look pretty. Come now, give me your comb and, here, take my blue hairpin." Elsie shook her head at Susannah's look of objection. "Nope, it's yours, a wedding present."

Susannah gave her an exasperated look, but Elsie insisted, stating that the Bridges were not even here yet. So, Susannah pulled her wooden comb out of the carpet bag and let her cousin take her hair down and arrange the dark rolling tendrils around her shoulders, sweeping the front sides up and securing them with a sparkly beaded hairpin pulled from Elsie's hair.

Susannah complained that she had never worn her hair so impractically, but Elsie insisted that this was a wedding and it was ok to be a bit frivolous. Susannah retorted that she was putting her hair straight back up afterward, and the girls giggled together one last time before the Bridges family entered and brushed by them without a word, smothering the cheerful mood. She watched as her uncle explained the change in brides to Mr. Bridges and the rotund gray-haired man nodded and shook hands with Byron.

Traveling along the side wall, Susannah made her way to the front of the small auditorium that doubled as a school house during the week. She did not take her eyes off the family that she was joining herself to. Mr. Bridges, the banker, was looking as pompous as always, overdressed in his fancy suit, with the gold watch and chain showing. His mustache was carefully curled and he wore a look of arrogant frustration. His wife sat at his side, pure satisfaction on her puffy face. She looked like a cat that had just eaten a mouse. She always looked like that when she had gotten her way. Jeffrey, on the other hand, did not match either of his parents. He stood at the front of the room, his arms bent together over his heart, in a pout that was almost an exact copy of Aunt Jane's. His handsome features were drawn together in an ugly scowl. Susannah had never seen someone look so much like they did not want to be somewhere. The feeling was almost palpable. It exuded from him like steam escaping under the lid of a boiling pot. She sure hoped he would not explode, or boil over on her, when this was all done. She shook herself, she had known him in passing for half her life. He was not known to be mean or violent. Nothing else really mattered. The husband part of this arrangement was incidental. Jeff was just a means to an end. She stepped almost happily to the front to join him, eager to finally leave this town, as she had wanted to for so, so long.

The tall preacher stepped forward and asked them all to bow their heads and pray. He prayed for the new couple to be blessed in their life together and to never stray from God's path. He asked that they might always treat each other with kindness and love. When the prayer was finished, he cleared his throat and launched into his usual fancy phrases in a ringing voice that echoed off the walls. Susannah heard "dearly beloved", "this man and this woman shall be joined together for life", and many more rehearsed platitudes. Finally, he seemed to remember that she and Jeff were standing there. He looked down at them. Susannah glanced at her groom and wondered if he ever planned to unfold his arms. He hadn't yet looked at her, not once.

Upon seeing the emotions in their eyes, Jeff's angry, Susannah's calm and indifferent, the preacher seemed to pause. He grew more serious and began to direct his questions to them and seemed to be truly focused on their answers.

"Do you, Jeffrey, take this woman to be your wedded wife? To have and to hold, from this day forward, for better for worse, for richer for poorer, in sickness and in health, all the days of your life?"

There was a pause and for the first time, Jeffrey actually turned and glanced at her. His eyes widened for a moment, then the scowl returned. He took a breath and said simply, "Yes."

The preacher looked a little startled, but given Jeffrey's unhappy demeanor, he decided not to correct him by asking him to say the traditional "I do". Instead he turned to Susannah and repeated the question.

"And do you, Susannah, take this man to be your wedded husband? To have and to hold, from this day forward, for better for worse, for richer for poorer, in sickness and in health, all the days of your life?"

Susannah said clearly, "I do.", and immediately a strange shiver shimmied up her spine. She shook it off. Her cheeks grew a little hot with anticipation. Her life was about to change. Finally. Who knew what the future might hold. It was wonderful to be out of the monotonous predictable world of her uncle's farm and actually not know what was coming next. She had not felt that wondering, that eager curiosity, in so long. It might have overwhelmed her if it was not lessened by how self conscious she felt standing up there in front of everyone.

"Now," the preacher continued, "Repeat after me. I, Jeffrey Bridges, pledge to be faithful and true to you, Susannah Kelly, until death. This is my solemn vow."

Jeff turned and looked at the preacher. His expression seemed a combination of pained and startled. His arms finally fell to his sides. He glanced at his parents, looked up at the ceiling, and then finally looked back at Susannah. Watching him and seeing his discomfort, Susannah suddenly felt that she wanted to help him. It was her nature to give whatever aid she could to anyone in need. Without thinking about it, she abruptly stepped forward and took his fingertips in hers. The slight pressure and kind gestures seemed to steady him. "Our choice," she whispered, low enough that no one else could hear. Was she giving him a chance to back out? Would he take it? She tried not to explore the devastation of this lost opportunity if he did. Out of the corner of her eye, she thought she saw Aunt Jane lean forward a little, hopeful, like maybe she would not lose her servant after all.

Jeffrey stared into Susannah's eyes. His brows drew together in contemplation and then without taking his gaze off her warm green eyes, he spoke softly, "I, Jeffrey Bridges, pledge to be faithful and true to you, Susannah Kelly, until death. This is my solemn vow." She smiled at him and he seemed transfixed for a moment and then, all of a sudden, the angry frown returned. He dropped her hands and stepped back, staring at the floor.

Susannah did not care that he had pulled away from her. He had gone through with his part of the ceremony. Her dreams were intact. This was going to happen. She turned eagerly toward the preacher to seal this commitment, once and for all, with her own last vow.

The preacher told her what to say and she looked at her groom and gave him her promise without hesitation. "I, Susannah Kelly, pledge to be faithful and true to you, Jeffrey Bridges, until death. This is my solemn vow."

The preacher drew himself up to his full height and raised his voice. "I now present to you, Mr. and Mrs. Jeffrey Bridges." He looked at Jeff. "You may now kiss your bride."

"No, thank you," Jeffrey said, pressing his lips together, and turning to leave.

The preacher caught him mid-stride, by putting his arm around his shoulders. "Not so fast, young man, you still have to sign the license."

"Fine, let's get this over with." Jeffrey strode to the nearby side table, scrawled his name in the appropriate places and then stomped out of the building. His mother jumped up and followed him.

Susannah was not bothered by her new husband's bad mood. He chose this, the same as she had, and all she could think about was that she never had to bow and scrape to petty Aunt Jane ever again. She was free, free, free. Yes, life would not be perfect with that fuming boy as her husband and a big, challenging future ahead, but it was all hers. *Her* new life. *Her* unknown possibilities. *Her* bright new road spreading out before her. She was so excited that she thought nothing could bring her spirits down.

She happily signed the licenses and accepted the copy the preacher gave her. Then she was smothered in hugs from her younger cousins. She whispered words of love and promises of the future to them and then they were ushered out of the church by their father. He had just come over, after another handshake with Mr. Bridges. "Well, it's all set," he said. "The farm is safe. You go on now, Sue. Best wishes and so forth." Byron barely patted her on the shoulder and then just left. Just like that. The only father figure she had had for a decade and that was all he said to her as they parted ways forever. She blinked and shook it off. She could expect no more from him.

That left only Aunt Jane and Elsie. The three of them stood alone in the church foyer, looking at each other, while Susannah quickly repinned her hair back up into a simple bun. This had all happened so fast. Susannah was reeling a little. She was not used to whirlwind days, giant forever goodbyes, or massive life changes. It left her a little lightheaded.

Elsie was all smiles. She wrapped her arm around Susannah's waist and said, "Best wishes, Susie!" She squeezed her cousin excitedly. "Oh, I'm so happy for you!"

Jane, on the other hand, had a sour look on her face. She seemed to have finally resigned herself to the fact that this was happening and there was nothing she could do about it now. "Don't know what y'all have to be so happy about. She barely knows that boy." She looked right at Susannah. "I mean, have you ever even spoken to him before today?" She shook her head back and forth. "You're gonna be worse off than me when my Pa put his foot down and made me marry Byron, and you can see how that turned out. Why, Susannah, you don't know what you're in for. You ain't got nothin' to be so all-fired happy about… and goin' off and leaving me in the lurch…" Her voice trailed off.

Jane's negative words made Susannah's shy smile droop. Her fluttering heart, filled with excitement, began to settle. What was she getting herself into? Was Jane right? Her aunt sure knew how to throw a damper over an occasion, but Elsie was not to be deterred. She tightened her grip on Susannah's waist.

"Come now, Ma," Elsie said brightly, with a purposefully forced cheerfulness. "Susannah is about to embark upon a grand adventure. A brand new life. She might as well do so with high hopes, right? Don't you remember what it was like to start fresh? Your whole future ahead of you?"

"I try not to remember," Elsie's mother mumbled. Then she sighed and glared at Susannah. "Well, I suppose I should wish you well, even though you're abandoning me to do all your work, after everything we've done for you. Elsie will be gone soon too, so just what am I supposed to do?"

Susannah opened her mouth to say her customary apology.

That usually helped to keep the peace between herself and her aunt, but she suddenly realized that she didn't have to. Her mouth slowly closed. There was no more need to appease Jane. Susannah smiled sweetly and tried to think of a way to return kindness for Aunt Jane's selfishness. She opened her mouth again, little flickers of excitement returning as she realized she might never have to see Aunt Jane again after this moment.

"Oh, Auntie," Susannah said kindly, "Marigold and Jessica will be a big help to you now. They're getting older and I've tau--...I mean, we've taught them lots about how to help you around the house and….and there will be two less mouths to cook for, and the boys aren't babies anymore. I'm sure you'll be all right. I'll… I'll be prayin' for you every day."

"Oh, Ma, don't be letting her go on so," Elsie rebuked, "When she's literally saving our farm and my marriage."

Jane pursed her lips for a moment and then muttered, "Well, thanks and all that, I guess." The words seemed to burn her lips. Not wanting to look at her niece any longer, she glanced around. Noticing that the rest of her family was gone, Jane headed for the door. "I'd best be going. Come along, Elsie…"

Susannah stared after her for a moment. The door closed and that was that. Jane was finally out of her life. It was an odd feeling. Susannah suddenly had an intense flash of worry for her family. She had practically been raising her cousins and running the house completely. What would happen to them now? Would Jane step up, finally? Well, she would have to. What was done, was done, and there was no going back now. Susannah had saved the farm and she had saved Elsie and Josh. She couldn't save everyone. She turned back to her cousin Elsie, her best friend in the world. Tears filled her eyes as she realized that she might never see her again.

Elsie enveloped her in a warm hug. "We'll write. We'll write lots! Don't fret. You'll get me to blubbering." She pulled back and looked into Susannah's face. "That boy will leave without you, so just get on now. The little ones and I love you, and we'll be ok. You go get that future you deserve."

"I...I love you, Elsie," Susannah said, taking a few steps backward. "I wish you a beautiful wedding. You write and tell me all about it." She was at the door now. Elsie was nodding. Susannah's hands found her bag and then the knob and she forced herself outside.

The bright sunshine warmed her and cleared her eyes of tears. She looked around and took in the small prairie schooner across the street in front of the general store. It was packed to the hilt, with various bumps and protrusions poking against the white cover from the inside. She realized, all of the sudden, that she must not keep her groom waiting. She quickened her pace.

Chapter 3

Jeffrey was approaching his wagon on the other side of the street from Susannah. He had a leather pouch in his hand and Susannah saw him climb up onto the wagon seat, lean over the back of it and tuck the pouch amongst the supplies in the front of the wagon.

As her new husband settled into a sitting position on the wagon seat, Susannah called out softly, as she crossed the street. "Are we ready to go?"

Jeff did not look at her. His eyes ran over his horses' tack, checking everything. "*I'm* ready to go, but there's no need for *you* to come."

Susannah stopped dead in her tracks only a step away from the wagon. She was used to people snapping unpleasant things at her and she usually responded with patient silence, but her silence now was more stunned than patient.

"Listen," he continued, forcing himself to finally turn and look at Susannah, "Your farm is safe now and my Pa kept the deal he made with me too, so we both got what we wanted. There's no need to take this any further."

Feeling her dreams slipping away, Susannah suppressed a tremble and managed to find her voice, "But....but, I'm your wife."

"I'm aware of that, but since I've never intended on having a wife, ever, having one far away won't make any difference to me, I'll never be with anyone else, so my plans can stay intact," he paused, nodding. "Yeah, it'll be like a long distance marriage....the kind where we never have to see each other again. It'll be fine, and you can go back to your farm."

"But, that's no marriage at all..." Susannah couldn't keep the shock out of her voice.

"Well, like I said, I never wanted a marriage!" Jeff's words were sharp. His eyes narrowed in anger. A few breaths passed in silence, then he continued, a bit softer. "Look, you can't possibly have wanted an arranged marriage either. I mean, how long have you even known about this? Two hours? Surely, you just want to go back home. It won't please my mother, but there's nothing she can do about it now."

"Home?" Susannah's knees were going weak. Every plan, every hope, was vanishing. She couldn't let this happen. She'd never have another chance. "I....I...don't have a home. I was going to build one....with...with you."

Jeff's chest fell a little at the pain on Susannah's face. "Look, I'm just saying that's what *I* want, but I guess I understand that a future where you could never marry might not be what *you* want....." His voice trailed off. He turned his eyes away from her, staring down the road, as if looking at his future too, watching it slip away just like Susannah was. He took a deep breath, steeling himself. "I understand that I'm your husband, and if I leave you here against your will, I'll be abandoning you, and, even though I never wanted to be a husband, I won't be that kind, one who abandons his wife, so I guess it's up to you, but," he turned his head back to look at her again, earnest begging in his eyes, "But I just thought you'd been roped into this, and would be happy to go home. Please, Ms. Kelly, I....I...mean, uh, Su-Susannah, it's Susannah, right? Please, say you want to go home, I'll even drive you there."

He waited, eyebrows arched in hope, staring down at her. Susannah gathered herself. Never in her life had she blatantly gone against the wishes of someone else. She always acquiesced if it was what was better for the other person, even if it hurt her, but for the first time in her life, she just couldn't do it. She couldn't. She was married to Jeff and would never be able to get out of this town, or have a family or home of her own. She was tied to him, which meant no other man could help her now, ever. A lifeless future as Aunt Jane's drudge, year after year, until she died old and miserable, flashed before her eyes. She blinked and cleared her throat.

"I'm sorry, Mr. Bridges, but, please, I….I have to go with you, please. I have to!" She stared up at him, squinting in the sunlight, waiting for his response, imploring him. "I…I can't stay in this town."

Turning his head away from her, Jeff let out a long sigh so filled with palpable disappointment that it seemed to roll off of him in waves almost visible to Susannah. His body sort of deflated into the wagon seat, as he sagged in displeasure. Reluctantly, he finally gathered the reins into his hands and glared ahead, not wanting to make eye contact with his wife.

"You'd better not *ever* be a bother to me, you hear?" His voice was angry and low, his brows drawn together in a dark grimace. "I think I've been very clear that I do *not* want a wife."

Susannah's stomach dipped at the sheer anger in Jeff's tone, she hung her head automatically, feeling very bad, but not bad enough to change her mind. She couldn't. "Yes," she whispered, "You've been very clear."

"Well, don't expect me to help you up. You are not *ever* to slow me down. Got it?" His voice was still very cold.

Susannah's head shot up. "Got it." She was not about to delay one second. It would only take a flick of his wrist to get that wagon going and leave her behind. Her uncle had never once helped her into a wagon and she was quite adept at not needing help with anything. She placed her bag in the floorboards, grabbed ahold of the seatback and swung herself up into the wagon in two quick movements, before Jeff could change his mind.

"Is that all you've got?" he said, nudging her small, half-filled bag with his foot.

"Yes." She picked up her bag and placed it on the other side of her feet.

"Well, I guess that's something," he mumbled.

"It won't get in your way and neither will I," Susannah stated clearly, looking into his face. "I'll be the quietest wife any man ever had. I'll never get in your way. You'll barely know I'm around. I...I promise...uh, Mr. Br—"

"Call me, Jeff," he interrupted, "But you'd best not be calling me nothin' hardly ever, since you're going to be quieter than a church mouse, as you said, right?"

"Right." She nodded, clamping her lips closed tight.

"I'll be holding you to that."

Turning his face back to the front again, he set his jaw, shook the reins and headed forward. The town began to move slowly away and Susannah was not sad to see it go. She had never been happy here with an aunt and uncle who had never wanted her and didn't appreciate her. She had taught herself not to be hurt by their inability to feel love or gratefulness and she was proud of the way she had handled herself all these years, but it was no way to live for the rest of her life. Susannah watched eagerly as the buildings disappeared, giving way to a long road with endless prairie on both sides. She did not look back. She never wanted to see Seagleton again. The further away they got, the more she relaxed. This was really happening. She was truly getting away. She was married. She was off to her new life. She didn't care that Jeff didn't want her, she didn't really want him either. He was just her ticket out of her circumstances, her means to an end, her ride towards her dreams. She would be no burden to him. He could have whatever he wanted from her. She would be a good wife to him. She was ready for whatever path he took her on, as long as it was away from her old life.

***

Hours went by in complete silence as the wagon rumbled along the well-worn road heading northwest. Finally, when the sun was high in the middle of the sky, Jeff stopped the wagon and spoke for the first time since leaving Seagleton.

"So, I've been thinking of a new plan. I want to be on my own and you want to be somewhere new, so….," he gestured towards the left. Susannah could see that they were at a crossroads. Soon she would realize it was a figurative one, as well as a literal one. The dirt road forked off in four directions, but she didn't know why Jeff was pointing that out. She looked at him with a question in her eyes. "Collingsworth is that way," he continued, pointing more adamantly southwest. "It's only a day's travel. We could be there by dinnertime tomorrow."

Susannah knew Collingsworth was in that direction, though she had never been there. Why was Jeff stopping here to tell her this? She remained quiet, waiting for him to explain.

"It's a nice town, twice as big as Seagleton," Jeff went on, hope slowly entering his voice. "They have lots of opportunity for good jobs, even for a woman alone. There are two restaurants, a hotel, and plenty of shops. Why, the last time I was there, the tailor shop was looking for a seamstress and offering a room above the shop to live in. Something like that would be perfect for you. I don't mind the detour if it gets--," he bit his tongue short of saying , "gets you out of my hair".

Susannah remained quiet, but panic was rising in her throat. Jeffrey could see her resistance to the idea written all over her face. The newfound hope drained out of his voice and it took on a pleading tone. "Susannah, this way we can both have the life we want."

He was looking at her so imploringly. His eyes bore into her. "But that's not the life I want…." she mumbled. "I…I want a house with a kitchen and garden. Little places to call my own, in some pretty open country somewhere. That's all I'm asking for, it's not too much, is it, Jeff? I promise you, I'll make your home a cozy place for you..." Her breath caught as she struggled not to let him see the tears of fear forming in her eyes. Her voice lowered to a whisper. "Please, don't leave me in some strange town, all alone, where my marriage to you will prevent any other man from ever taking me out of there...., please, Jeff."

She couldn't believe the turn this day was taking. The options Jeffrey presented had not occurred to her when she had agreed to marry him this morning. How could things be going so wrong?

Jeffrey's anger was returning. He slapped his thigh with his fist. "It could be a good life for you!" he insisted. "In fact if you want a bigger, more exciting place, I'm even willing to drive you all the way to Dodge City, if it'll get my plans back on track. Please, just say 'yes', Susannah."

The second offer was even less appealing. Dodge City, Kansas, was over a week's travel away and Susannah couldn't imagine a life in such a rough place, filled with saloons and rowdy dance halls. She tilted her head down and stared at her hands buried in her lap. It was hard to keep pushing what she wanted; she was so unaccustomed to it, but she forced her mouth to form the words. They came out deathly quiet. "I...I can't...say...yes...Jeff. I'm... sorry." She gulped air, afraid to look at him.

Jeff let out an angry grunt and jumped down from the wagon. She watched him pacing around, kicking at the dusty prairie grass. He tore off his hat and tossed it furiously into the air. Finally, he stood for a long time with his hands on his hips, gazing off across the prairie. Would he kick her out of the wagon, Susannah wondered? Would he drive to Collingsworth and leave her there against her will?

Susannah tensed as Jeffrey came storming back, circled the horses and stomped up to her side of the wagon. She promised herself that she wouldn't resist him any further. Standing up for herself for the first time, and doing it twice in one day, had taken all her strength, and seeing how miserable Jeff was took the wind right out of her determination. Susannah didn't feel hopeful or proud of herself. She just felt scared and worried. If he demanded that she not go further with him, she would have to go along with it. She couldn't fight him. She didn't have it in her. Taking a breath, she waited for what he was going to say next.

He shook a finger at her as she looked down at him. "All right, you listen to me, I'll not have my plans derailed, not one iota, by a woman I never wanted. Is that understood?" As he watched, Susannah nodded her understanding. He folded his arms angrily as if holding his temper in. "I've seen too much of how women are from my mother, and I've never wanted that kind of lazy, nagging annoyance in my life. So, if I see one shred of that kind of behavior from you—pestering me, complaining, needling your way into my every decision, and never doin' a lick of work--- I swear, whether you say yes or not, I'll drop you at the nearest town, and never look back." His hands went to his hips again and he glared at her. "You hear me?"

She nodded again. "Not all women are like that, Jeff," she said softly, suddenly feeling like she understood him a little better. "I...I'm not like that--"

"You'd just better not be." He stomped away to retrieve his hat.

Suddenly feeling concerned for him, not just for herself, Susannah called out quietly, "I'll never be anything but a help to you, Jeff.", but he did not respond. He simply grabbed his hat, stomped back to the wagon, climbed up and grabbed the reins. He sat there in silence for a moment, his shoulders heaving a little in frustration. Susannah looked at him. "I'll be a good wife to you," she whispered.

His brows came together angrily. "I don't *want* a wife," he muttered and shook the reins, urging the horses forward.

Susannah was still surprised at how adamant Jeffrey was about not wanting to be married. She had thought all young men wanted a wife for various reasons, even if just to share the work.

Susannah had seen a poor marriage. She knew what that world looked like, and she did not fear it. She didn't care about having love or even companionship. As she had said, she just wanted something to call her own. Susie had told her new husband the truth. All she wanted was a little kitchen and garden to keep clean and homey. These were her dreams, and whatever she had to give to this man she would give gratefully, if, in return, he would just give her the freedom to keep her own home and tend to her own little realm. Susannah was frightened now that Jeff might try again to get rid of her, that she might never have the simple things she wanted.

They were headed northwest again and Susannah relaxed, just a little, as the turn-off to Collingsworth slipped way, but she wondered how long it would be before she felt peaceful again. All kinds of new worries were beginning to swirl in her mind.

Chapter 4

As the hours went quietly by, Susannah began to relax. She had learned, over the years, to find the good in the bad parts of life. Back at the farm, she had learned not to dwell on the endless labor her aunt put her through, but rather to focus on how she was learning the skills a woman needed in life. She concentrated on good times with the children, instead of worrying over her aunt's constant scolding. If her hands ached from too much sewing, she thought only of the beauty of the garment she had completed and its usefulness to whichever family member she had made it for. If she had a fleeting wish not to be sleeping in a dusty barn loft, freezing in the winter and sweating in the summer, she focused on the perfect view of the stars through her loft window, unblurred by glass.

Now, Susannah turned her positivity skills on her new spouse. She glanced at him out of the corner of her eye. Besides the obvious handsomeness of his strong jaw, piercing blue eyes, and rich brown hair flecked with gold, it was hard to see anything good about him yet. Though she was not blind to them, Jeff's looks meant little to her. Kindness would have been far preferable, but she had resigned herself to marry a stranger and could not now complain over what she had gotten. She had known the risks. She reminded herself that she'd never heard of Jeff being cruel or violent, having heard about him and seen him around town for ten years, but the lack of any true evil in him did not necessarily make him a good companion. She didn't want a companion though, and was a little surprised that the word had entered her mind. She watched his hands as he drove the wagon and tried to tell herself that he had skills, but really she didn't know that. Anyone could drive a wagon, and she had no idea what else he might be capable of, if anything. She looked back at his face and it finally dawned on her. He had not left her, no matter how much he had wanted to. That had to mean that there was some honor in him. That was not nothing. She had found something good in him. It was a start.

She turned her eyes away, surprised at herself. In her planning for a husband, she had not believed that she would give much thought at all to finding good in this hypothetical person. She hadn't thought that she would contemplate him much further than how to do whatever work he needed her to do and the few others things that men wanted from women. It startled her that she even cared about getting to know and understand him. It was an unexpected twist in her plan, but then again what did she know? Her world had always been so small, how could she have foreseen what to expect as her life expanded into the unknown? Jeff wasn't imaginary and unnamed anymore, and that changed things, and would continue to change things in ways she could not anticipate. Susannah was beginning to feel a little disconcerted and confused, so she turned her eyes to the distant horizon and returned to more familiar thoughts: her dreams of a pleasant future home.

Jeff reached into a canvas bag under the seat and pulled out a small broken piece of hardtack. He munched on it, until it was gone. A few minutes later, a grouse fluttered out of the grasses on Susannah's side of the wagon, squealing at the approach of the large vehicle, and quickly disappearing back into the swaying plants. The movement and sound drew Jeff's attention and as he turned his head, he caught sight of his wife. Their gazes locked for a moment and Susannah could see a thought popping into Jeff's mind, widening his eyes. He suddenly reached into the canvas bag again and offered her a piece of hardtack too.

"I'm sorry," he mumbled, handing her his canteen as well.

31

She accepted the water and food. "Thank you," she whispered.

Jeff sighed. "It occurs to me now, that I haven't packed enough food for two people."

Susannah swallowed a nibble of the tough dry bread. "That's ok," she answered softly. "We'll make do."

Jeffrey turned and looked at her for a long moment, his eyes tilted in surprise, but he did not comment further.

Susannah was glad that her husband seemed to be resigning himself to her presence, after trying twice to get rid of her. She hoped he would not try again and she was glad to hear a voice from him that was not filled with anger. She promised herself to strive not to make him angry again, though she had learned long ago not to blame herself for the anger of others. Her aunt and uncle had there own problems, shortcomings that were their responsibility. It seemed that her new husband had issues of his own too. She must try not to feel guilty, when she had committed no crime. Jeffrey chose marriage. It wasn't Susannah's fault that that decision resulted in actually having a wife. If he'd gone into the deal assuming he could get out of it afterward, that was his mistake, not hers.

When the sun finally began to dip low in the sky, Jeff pulled the wagon off the trail and climbed down without a word. When Susannah saw him removing the hitching gear from the horses she determined they were setting up camp for the night. She climbed down and tried to think of something useful to do. She didn't want to bother Jeff, but she felt that doing anything without asking could make him angrier. It had been a long time since she had had to get to know someone. She still understood so little of what to expect from him.

"Um…Jeff? Shall I make supper? Or a fire? What would you like?" she fumbled, turning left and right, not sure if she should go to the back of the wagon for supplies. "I mean what do you have?"

"Stop asking me questions," Jeff blurted. "I knew it! I knew you'd be like this." He paused in his work, looked down at the ground and shook his head back and forth unhappily. Then he went back to lifting a leather line over the back of one of the horses. "I'm busy, ok?!"

He did not look at her and continued working. Susannah understood that he had dismissed her and she had better not speak again. She grabbed her bag and, slowly, went to the back of the wagon and just stood still a moment, trying to think of a way to be useful without doing anything that Jeff might disapprove of. Glancing at the bags and crates piled in the wagon bed, Susannah decided not to touch any of her husband's things without his permission. She began to stomp down a small area of grass behind the wagon with her feet, until she had created a small clearing. Then she set about tearing grass and twisting it into thick pieces that they could burn if Jeff wanted a fire.

As the sun began to set, Jeff ambled around to the back of the wagon to find Susannah sitting in a newly formed flat area, twisting grasses. Her hands were red and there was a pile of the twists beside her. Jeff couldn't quite define his feelings at seeing her like that. She was an enigma. Women were nothing but pure irritants, but he had never seen one work until her hands were sore, doing something useful that no one had told her to do.

"Hey," he said, "That's plenty. Here...," He handed her his flint and steel, from his pocket, and turned to gather a few things from the wagon.

Susannah tilted the grass twists into a teepee and pulled some fuzzy undergrowth from the base of the grasses near her. She reminded herself that next time she did this, she really should dig out her old garden gloves from her bag. She rolled the tinder into a large ball and held it in her hand. Placing the gray piece of flint on top of the bundle, she threaded her fingers through the C-shaped piece of steel and struck it against the flint three times. Quickly she blew on the tiny spark that had lit inside her hand, watching it grow. Then she deposited it at the base of the grass twists and watched a fire bloom. She looked up to see Jeff staring at her.

"My Ma never did that…," he mumbled, then shook himself out of his reverie. "Anyway, next time just use these. We've got more than enough."

He handed her several corn cobs and she poked them into the fire.

"Listen, I didn't bring no girl-food, ok? I spent every summer, since I was eight, driving cattle with my grandpa, and I just packed the same food we always had on the cattle drive, so that's just gonna have to be good enough for you."

Susannah nodded. "I'm sure that'll be just fine."

Jeff looked perplexed again. After a stunned moment, he reached for a small pot he had laid on the grass and leaned over to put it on the fire. "I was just plannin' on beans tonight…" he mumbled, concentrating on settling the pot at an angle where the handle would be out of the fire.

"Won't you let me cook them for you, Jeff?" Susannah said, staring at him.

He stared back. She was sitting on her knees on the dirty ground, her skirt wrapped under her legs. At some point, she had pulled an apron out of her bag and tied it around her waist. Now, she just sat still, her hands buried in her lap, staring at him.

"Well, I….," Jeff had never felt so at a loss. This girl kept surprising him. He couldn't remember a time his mother ever asked to be allowed to do any work. "I suppose if you're going to be here, you'd best be useful. I mean that is what I…I…um… I told you this morning, so….you just, uh…," he rose to his feet and stepped away, "You go ahead, but just a handful, mind you, we aren't made of money and won't be stoppin' for more…uh… more beans." He had reached the wagon and leaned one hand against it.

"Yes, Jeff." Susannah nodded again, reaching for the single tin cup that her husband had laid nearby, she looked up when he spoke again.

"Of course, I....," Jeff sounded a little sheepish, "I mean two handfuls, one for you and one...uh..for me."

"Ok," Susannah said, softly, filling the tin cup with water from the barrel Jeff had brought over while she made the fire.

She poured two cupfuls into the pot and looked up to see Jeff lighting a lantern. As he checked over the wagon, examining the wheels and retying various ropes, Susannah dropped two handfuls of beans into the pot, from the bag of dried beans Jeff had set in the clearing, and sprinkled in a pinch of salt from another bag he had left nearby. Jeff carried water barrels to the horses as Susannah stirred the beans, watching them boil. Now that she knew there were dried beans in the wagon, she would see to it that a portion was left soaking before tomorrow. It would help them cook faster next time. Jeff seemed to know it would take the beans a while to soften, as he busied himself for a long time before returning to the clearing. He was not eager to return to his wife's company.

Finally, Susannah sipped water from the tin cup as Jeff ate his beans, then he gave her the plate, having left half the beans for her. He took a drink of water and stared off across the shadowy blowing grasses.

"We've got some jerky too and coffee..." His voice trailed off and then he let out a slow resigned sigh and turned to look directly at her. "All right, look, ain't no point in beatin' around the bush, we don't have enough of nothin' for two people and that's the long and short of it."

"I...I'm sorry, Jeff," Susannah stuttered, unsure what else to say.

Jeff's brows came together in frustration. "Well, it wasn't your doin', it was mine!" He sighed again and settled himself more comfortably on the ground. He stretched his neck from side to side, thinking, then took a few breaths, calming his body and voice. When he spoke again, his tone was softer than Susannah had heard it before. "Listen, I know I've been cantankerous today...I...was....you know,... mad at the world! But that don't mean that you gotta go apologizin' for things that ain't your fault."

"I...I guess I'm just used to it," Susannah whispered, taking a bite of warm beans.

"Well, get unused to it, 'cause I don't like it." Jeff's voice had grown acerbic again.

"Ok, I'll try," Susannah responded, turning her eyes downward.

"Oh, for Pete's sake! I am no good at all this talkin'. I don't mean to fuss at you so much I...." A confused look crossed his face and he gave up, clamping his mouth shut and glaring down at the fire.

Susannah's habit of always wanting to help flared up. "We can make do with whatever food we've got, Jeff," she said softly, looking up at him, concern in her eyes. "I really don't eat much. I told you I won't be a bother to you and I meant it."

"Susannah," he responded softly, "We don't have enough water barrels. I'm not familiar enough with this route to risk not havin' enough water. There are supposed to be some long stretches ahead with nowhere to refill. I guess I...shouldn't have...presumed...." He stared out again across the twilight prairie. "It's my own fault. I was so furious with my Pa for forcin' me, but I still shouldn't have agreed to marry and just assumed I could get out of it, and that you'd want to stay behind. I...I...I... well, I assumed too much. I've had all day to calm down and I....I guess I can see that now." He looked down at the empty tin cup in his hands. "This ain't what I wanted, but that's life, and I reckon we'd best just pick up a few things at the next town...." His voice faded away, filled with unhappiness.

"Can I ask....," she hesitated.

He did not look up. "Go ahead, might as well...," he mumbled.

"Well, why did you get married, Jeff? What happened with you and your father?" She was looking at him now, wanting to understand him.

He suddenly looked right into her eyes and just stared for a moment. Then he tilted his head, as if having a sudden idea. "Your aunt and uncle, they...uh...they weren't that nice to ya, were they, Susannah?"

Embarrassed, without really knowing why, Susannah's eyes turned downward again and her voice lowered. "They.....they never hurt me."

Jeffrey nodded in understanding. "That isn't really the same thing as being nice, though, is it?" He nodded again. "Yeah, that's kind of how my folks were. We never got along. Never saw eye to eye, not with my pa or my ma. That's why they packed me off to my grandfather's ranch every summer, to get rid of me, but it was the best thing they ever did for me. Because of my time there, I learned to be a cattleman and all I've ever wanted was to have my own ranch, far from my folks." He grabbed a large handful of grass and used it to wipe out the bean residue from the pot as he continued. "Homesteadin' is only for farmers. I knew if I wanted to raise cattle instead of crops, that I'd have to buy the land outright. So, I saved for years, since I was little. Every odd job I could get until I was older and started lookin' for real work. Then Pa started to realize I wasn't going to follow in his footsteps and he got real ornery about it, wanted me to work in the bank like he'd always planned, but I refused. Finally, he said if I worked in the bank until I had half of my start-up money, he'd give me a bank loan for the rest with no interest. 'Course he thought he was going to make me like banking and I'd never wanna leave, but that was never going to happen." Jeff smiled a little, but the smile faded fast. "Anyway, I didn't really want to agree to it, but I knew if I tried to earn enough on my own it was going to take years and years and half my life would be gone. The salary from the bank was so much better than any other job I could find around town...." Jeff stopped talking for a moment, memories flowing through his mind. "So, long story short, I worked in that stuffy bank of his from when I was fourteen until I turned twenty last week, saved enough to finally get out of there, and I was all ready to go yesterday, had the wagon packed and everything, when my ma up and decided that I couldn't go without a wife. She actually called me a fool right to my face." He nodded at Susannah's shocked expression. "She knew I never intended to be married and she has always had a way of injecting misery wherever she could find a place to wedge in her opinions, her insults…" He shook himself a little, stopping the thought in its tracks. His voice had been growing angry again and he took a sip of water and calmed down. "Well, when she puts her foot down, Pa has never been able to stand against her. He's never really worn the pants, so to speak, around my house, and that's probably why I've striven so hard to be nothing like him---why I refused to ever let a woman walk all over me like….," he paused, looking right at Susannah. "Well, anyway, he was supposed to give me the money he promised me this morning, the money that I'll need to buy my land and my first herd and to get settled on my ranch, and basically, he went back on his word, he just flat out refused to give me a dime until my mother was appeased." Silence fell in the tiny clearing. Susannah was shocked, but then she supposed it was no worse than what Uncle Byron had agreed to, practically selling his daughter to save his farm. "So…um…," Jeff continued, "You know the rest."

Susannah didn't know what to say. Part of her felt for Jeff's predicament and almost wanted to let him off the hook his parents had put him on, but images of what her life would be like if she gave him what he wanted and let him leave her in some town somewhere, never to marry again, never to have a home of her own, kept her from speaking. She just nodded and stayed quiet until Jeff got his bedroll from the wagon and began to arrange it on the opposite side of the fire from her. After a moment, he looked up and caught Susannah, sitting very still, staring at him.

He cleared his throat. "If you thought that....uh...that something was going to happen...um... between us tonight, well, you can just think again because---"

"You don't want me. I know, Jeff," Susannah whispered.

Susannah's voice was solemn, soft, it almost blew away on the wind. Her eyes were boring into him. She made him feel very strange.

He realized something all of a sudden and it just fell out of his mouth, "It's not you, you, Susannah....I mean....it's....it's not you, specifically."

"I know," she sighed gently, "You don't want a wife at all. Any wife."

"Exactly," he stared at her. "It's not that I hate women. I don't hate anybody. I don't even hate my parents. I tried that for a while, when I was younger. It was a waste. Didn't hurt anybody, but me..."

"Yeah, I've been there," Susannah nodded, slipping her apron off and putting it back in her carpet bag. "Goodnight, Jeff," she whispered, settling down, with her head on her carpet bag, like a pillow.

"Um...goodnight, Susannah."

Jeff and Susannah, both, drifted off to sleep, on their first night as husband and wife, with a thousand conflicting plans and worries rushing around in their minds.

Chapter 5

For the next few days, Susannah spent endless hours in thought. Jeff seemed to regret opening up to her on their first night. He was in a bad mood most of the time and barely spoke to her, though he did tell her she could do the cooking however she saw fit, as long as she made the food last. That gave her a little something to do, but there wasn't much that could be done with beans and jerky. She was careful not to use too much of anything and kept trying to settle her mind. She could no longer see a clear path ahead.

Susannah was trying to figure out exactly what to do with herself, what to focus on. There were a few options, including changing her mind and planning some kind of life in a town somewhere, but she grew very grim every time she considered it. She pictured loneliness, hardship and lack of purpose. She imagined the pain of never getting her simple dream of having something small of her very own, a kitchen and a garden in the country, with nature all around her, far from busy noisy towns. Finally, after observing Jeff and thinking about his past and his future, she decided on a course. Jeff's life would be far better than he had ever planned on, if she could quietly show him how nice it could be to have a good wife. She had never intended to give her imagined husband such consideration, but she was beginning to see how selfish that had been. She needed to devote her life to more than just her own happiness. So, she determined that she would concentrate on making Jeffrey happy, in ways he didn't think were possible. She would show him that not all women were like his mother, and hopefully along the way, she would get her own dreams as well. As she worked to build Jeff's home, she would be building her own home too.

She felt much better, after settling on a new path. She had something to focus on each day, something to think about and make little plans for. Her new goal kept her mind busy and helped her to feel more at ease. It motivated her and filled her with purpose and hope. She tried not to dwell on the fact that she had no idea how to make Jeff happy. She had to believe that she would learn as she went.

***

Unfortunately, Susannah did not learn as much as she would have liked in those first few weeks. She grew very confused about Jeff and about her future. She was very quiet, like her new husband wanted. It was in her nature to be so, but it did not make him happy. He glared at her a lot, and spoke to her so little, that she began to feel lonelier than she had ever felt before. It brought back those awful days on the stagecoach after her parents had died in a wagon accident. The neighbors had sold what few belongings her parents had had, that didn't belong to the bank, to buy the ten-year-old girl a ticket to her uncle's town. Susannah had spent a week, grieving alone with strangers, in that bumpy dusty carriage. It was the oddest sensation, feeling so alone while surrounded by people. It was one thing she had never felt in Seagleton. Her family had problems, but Elsie and the children made it impossible to feel lonely. Now, however, she recalled what it was like to be alone right next to someone. Jeffrey was there, but he wasn't really with her. Every time he looked at her, it was like his eyes were saying he didn't want her there. This was not what she had planned for when she had imagined escaping her circumstances by marrying. She had thought a man would find her who actually wanted a wife. She had told herself, in the beginning, that it was ok because she didn't want him either, but that was an easier thought when she was in the midst of the whirlwind of desperation to get out of her aunt and uncle's house, mixed with rosy dreams of a new future. It had all been so fresh, so overwhelming. Now that things were calm and far too deathly quiet, she began to feel the blush fading off the rose of possibility. Susannah's hopefulness was weakening and not being wanted, not even as a worker, or a friend, was starting to hurt.

The young bride told herself to be patient. A new life was coming. She filled her mind with pictures of her possible future. She thought of a cozy log cabin with a kitchen table constantly covered with flour from her baking, a charming little well in a breezy farmyard filled with the sound of chickens, a garden of neat rows and bright vegetables, all surrounded by some kind of large wild place. Perhaps it would be woods or endless prairie. Perhaps she would look out a tiny window every morning to see a herd of cattle moving on the horizon. Her imagination comforted her for hours, but she was always brought back to reality soon enough, whenever her eyes caught sight of Jeffrey.

She tried very hard to focus on her new goal, to find ways to make him happy, to make Jeff see that a wife was a good thing, just like it said in the book of Proverbs. She helped put things back into the wagon each morning without being asked. She arranged soft beds of grasses beneath his bedroll before he came to supper. When they reached a brook, she washed their extra clothes, as well as towels and blankets, hung them up to dry, then folded them and put them away. She flavored their beans with tasty herbs she found growing in the grasslands around them, and cut and folded their beef jerky into interesting shapes or softened it in the beans to make stew. She made sure his cup was filled with hot coffee before he awoke each day. When the morning was chilly, or the afternoon was filled with rain, she did not utter a word of complaint, but nothing she did seemed to matter to Jeff. He did not notice her efforts and, for weeks, they never had a real conversation like they had had that first night.

Jeff did not snap at her, or get as furious as he had been after the wedding, so she finally decided to take that as progress and she began to count the days until they reached their destination, even though she didn't know how many days that would be. Susannah had to believe that life would be better when they got there, wherever 'there' was, and that when she had a home to keep she would truly be able to show her husband that a wife could make his life better.

Eventually, they arrived at a dry little town, with hot wind blowing dirt down the one street. Spring didn't seem to know this place. There was not a flower or a green plant in sight. Susannah had mixed feelings. Part of her was thrilled to finally break the monotony of the journey with the sights and sounds of a new place, but the other part of her scrambled for how best to behave here. She had not experienced any true conflict with Jeff in well over two weeks and she worried that this new place would produce problems between them. Would she say or do something to upset him? Was she underestimating him? Was it possible that the anger of that first day was less of a true measure of his personality than the quiet sullen acceptance of the following weeks? It was so hard to figure him out. Had he resigned himself to her presence, truly? Or did he still want to get rid of her?

"Well, this place ain't much to look at." Jeff's voice startled Susannah. It was the first words he'd spoken all day. "We won't stay," he continued. "Don't reckon I'll even unhitch the horses. Just a quick stop at the general store up ahead. That's all we need."

Susannah looked around. They were rolling past a livery and a small blacksmith's shed. There was a saloon a ways in front of them, across the street from a faded building with a sign that read "General Store". There wasn't much more around, not even wooden sidewalks or a church building. Susannah felt the slight lurch as Jeffrey pulled back on the reins and the wagon stopped.

He sat there a moment. "We need a blanket for you and more barrels for water and I suppose you'll be wanting a bunch of stuff for cooking?" He looked at her.

She opened her mouth, unsure what to say, finally she just said, "No, Jeff. Whatever you think…"

Jeff sighed. "I guess I'm sayin' I don't rightly know what we need, Susannah. I never planned on…." He looked away.

"On havin' me along," she finished for him. "Look, we can just get a few more beans and we'll do fine, but would you….um….would you like anything else, Jeff?"

"Well, the hardtack isn't going to last all the way till we get there, but I don't want to be spending too much money right now. It's all allotted for things we'll need when we get settled and, you know, for the herd."

Susannah liked the way he kept saying "we". "Um…well, how about some cornmeal. I can make lots of things out of that, especially since we already have salt."

Jeff's eyes lit up, surprising Susannah. She found that she liked to see her husband's face brighten. It was the first time she had witnessed it.

"Can you make corn dodgers?" he was saying, "They're, uh… they're my favorite."

"Sure," Susannah smiled, "If I had some bacon grease—or just butter, I could make it with butter if they have some, and that will mean I can make johnnycakes too."

"Well, that's settled, then." Jeff dropped the reins. "We'll get you a bedroll, and we'll get two new water barrels, some cornmeal and see if they have butter. That shouldn't cost us too much."

He climbed down as he talked, but Susannah did not move. She was unsure what she should do. Jeffrey had parked in front of the general store. He walked around to Susannah's side, surveying the town. He looked up and down the street, watching the eyes of still people and listening to the whistle of unfriendly wind whipping around the corners of old buildings.

He shook his head back and forth. "I don't like the looks of this place," he said quietly. "Like I said, we'd best not stay long and we'll not go tellin' people where we're goin' neither." He stepped back towards the store, then stopped and turned around. "Well? Aren't you coming?"

"I…um…do you want me to?" Susannah looked right into his eyes.

He sighed slowly and stepped closer to her, looking up at her confused face. "I've made it hard for you, haven't I? You never know what to do." They stared at each other a moment, until he reached out his hands and said, "Come on, Susannah."

He lifted her out of the wagon. She liked the feel of his hands on her waist. It was the first time he had touched her since she grabbed him at their wedding. She was surprised at how gentle he was.

"I'm going to make our purchases quickly," he said, walking towards the store again. "I want you to watch our wagon out the window and let me know if anyone approaches it."

They climbed up onto a sort of long porch running the length of the general store's front. There was a thin man, with a scruffy beard, leaning against one of the support poles. He looked up when the couple approached.

"Well, what have we here?" He stepped towards them, blocking their way to the door. They could smell liquor on his breath. His eyes started running up and down Susannah's body. "Ain't you a perty little thing. Why, just look at that fiery hair of yours---"

Jeff angled himself half in front of Susannah, took her by the elbow and pushed past the man into the store.

"I was just tryin' to say it's always nice to have new blood around these parts," the man called out after them, as the door closed in his face.

With his jaw set and his tone grim, Jeff asked the storekeeper if he knew a water source nearby. First, the man said there was a well down the road. When he went on to say there was also a stream to the southeast, Jeff did not tell him that was the opposite of the way they were headed. He bought a cheap woolen blanket, ten pounds of beans, two water barrels, twenty pounds of cornmeal and then asked about butter.

"My wife makes it fresh every day," the gray-haired proprietor said as he stuffed several blocks of butter, wrapped in brown paper, into a small burlap bag. "Most folks around here don't have a cow, so we sell plenty of the stuff. Can't seem to sell the molasses, though. Got an extra shipment by accident. Too much for folks to buy. It's on sale…." He looked hopefully at Jeff.

Jeff glanced at Susannah. She was staying close to his side, but her back was too him. She was watching the wagon through the grimy front window. Jeff glanced at the wagon, then back at the old man.

"Uh, sure, I actually would like some molasses. Just one jug."

Finally, he paid from the leather pouch Susannah had seen him hide on their wedding day, and they headed out. Jeff carried the empty barrels with one under his arm and the other with the rim gripped in the same hand. The heavy sacks of cornmeal and beans were over his other shoulder. Susannah walked behind him with the new bedroll, jug of molasses and the bag of butter. She waited while he packed his items into the back of the wagon and poked the pouch deep inside the piles of supplies. As he positioned everything, Susannah looked around. She noticed the rude man from before had crossed the street and now stood in front of a saloon. His eyes followed the pouch from Jeff's hands right into the back of the wagon. When Susannah looked back at the wagon, Jeff was gone.

He had headed up front and was calling out to her. "I saw the well at the end of the street, we'll fill up our barrels on the way out."

Susannah leaned far into the covering of the wagon to tuck away the items in her hands. She used her body to block the view of the man across the street as she quickly found a place for everything, fiddled with the collar of her dress, and hurried up to the front of the wagon. She was surprised to see Jeff waiting to help her up.

As they pulled off down the road, Jeff looked at her. "I'm sorry, I never helped you in and out of the wagon, Susannah. I know you can do it yourself, but still. It was…. petty."

"That's all right," Susannah smiled at him, patting his arm reassuringly.

Jeff would not have said it out loud, but his wife's smile was breathtaking. It was all he could do not to gasp in awe. He cleared his throat and turned his gaze back to the road. This woman was starting to get under his skin and he didn't like it. He had never wanted her around and he still didn't. Right? He shook himself a little. Or course he didn't. She was a hassle. Look at how he'd had to push past that guy because of her and buy that blanket and all that food. She was always going to be in the way, nothing but a bother. A scowl began to fill his face. What had he been thinking, apologizing to her a moment ago. He didn't want to be helping no woman in and out of the wagon a dozen times a day, did he? Although, he had liked the way she had felt in his arms, so soft and light and warm. How did she manage to smell good, after three weeks on the trail? He shook that thought away too, happy to be at the well with a job to do.

"Just stay here," he grumbled, jumping out of the wagon before it had hardly stopped.

He untied the eight water barrels from the sides of the wagon and rolled them to the well. It took a good while to fill them, but Jeff was glad of the work. It made him feel calm again.

He was tying the last rope around the final barrel, dreading having to climb back up next to his wife, when he felt something hard against his back. A chill ran up his spine.

Chapter 6

Jeff knew, immediately, that the cool object poking him was a gun barrel. He dropped the rope and moved his hands slowly upward. His mind pictured his own rifle, too far away under the wagon seat. His eyes automatically connected with Susannah's. She was six feet to his right, up on the wagon seat. She was bending around the side staring at him, her eyes as big as saucers. He didn't know what message to send her. How could he reassure her? He was not used to being responsible for someone else. Ashamed, he turned his eyes downward.

A familiar voice spoke out clearly. "You just back up real slow-like, now, Mister. Ain't nobody gotta die today."

Realizing it was the same bearded man who had been staring at his wife in front of the store, Jeff backed up slowly, his mind trying to think of how to get out of this predicament, but he had Susannah to worry about. She was a sitting duck up there in the wagon, for anyone who was a halfway good shot. Would she move fast enough if he told her to get down? He didn't know. He hadn't been trying to get to know her. Any other man might have known his wife better. They should be more in sync. He gritted his teeth, angry at himself for a dozen reasons.

Jeff turned slowly to face his attacker. The man's face was cold, his eyes far more calculating than Jeff had given him credit for. He was holding a six-shot revolver of some sort. It was small and fast. Jeff realized he had no chance. He had to do whatever the man wanted or he could shoot both him and his wife down before they could blink. Jeff glanced around. A few people watched from far down the street. There was no one nearby to help and he didn't think this was a very helpful kind of town. He had not seen a jail on the way in and doubted there was a sheriff who would come to his aid.

"What do you want?" Jeff asked, keeping his voice low and calm.

"Hmmm," the man replied, "I believe I'd like to take that pouch of money off your hands. You know, the one I saw you put in the back of your wagon."

Jeff's shoulders drooped involuntarily and his face fell. In one flash, he saw his whole future crashing down around him. The pouch contained all his cash. How could he have been so foolish as to keep it all in one place?

"Well?" the man demanded, jiggling his gun a little. "What's it gonna be? I'm sure not gonna go digging around for it, so how 'bout you just go and get for me. Now!"

The man's voice had turned sharp, startling Jeff. He resisted a flinch. He hesitated. There had to be some way to get out of this without giving the man all his money. He fumbled to buy time.

"I'm a….not..not a rich man," Jeff muttered, "There's not as much money as you're hopin' for, I'm sure… and I…we…we need what we've got. Please, uh--"

"You're stalling." The thin man's voice had grown angrier. "But ain't no point. Nobody 'round here's gonna come to your rescue. Ain't a lawman for a hundred miles, and you know I'm not a very patient fellow…." He took three fast steps closer to Susannah, redirecting his gun's aim right at her. "So, how's about you get me what I want, or I'll just shoot your wife, how's that? Or you know what, I'll just take her as compensation for not getting my money!!" The man was shouting now. "Go!!"

Both Jeff and Susannah jumped. Jeff's heart was in his throat. He had known that woman was going to be nothing but trouble. If she had not been here, maybe he could have jumped this guy or something. She was costing him everything. No! He stomped that thought away. It was the robber who was costing him everything, not her, and he couldn't let anything happen to another human being, even some irritating unwanted wife, over money. He turned back toward the wagon. The other man was slowly backing away to a position where he could shoot either of them and still see what Jeff was doing. Jeff walked to the back, rooted around a little, and pulled out the pouch.

The man was walking back towards him and Jeff took the time to walk to the front of the wagon, on the same side the robber was on, which was Susannah's side. She scooted over on the seat, making room for him. He took ahold of the wagonseat with one hand, holding the pouch in the other.

"There's no need to waste any of your bullets," he said to the other man. "Just let us go."

He dropped the pouch on the ground halfway between them. When the man went for it, Jeff swung himself up into the wagon in one fluid motion and heard Susannah shake the reins. The horses walked forward and Jeff kept his eyes on the man. He had holstered his gun, clearly not planning on shooting them. Jeff grabbed the reins from Susannah and urged the horses faster and then, a moment later, even faster. They headed right out of town, going the wrong direction. They'd circle around later, and hopefully no one would know which way they had gone.

Furious over what had just happened, Jeff scooted back towards his normal spot on the left side of the wagon. "You keep your eye out," he ordered.

Susannah jumped up, crawled under the reins in front of his legs and leaned out the right side of the wagon, staring back at the town.

"No one's comin'," she said, softly. Then she waited several minutes, while they went over a few thousand yards of swaying grass, leaving the town far behind. Finally, she sat down. "No, he uh…he isn't followin'."

Things grew very quiet. There was nothing but the sound of the horses' hooves and the rumbling of the wagon. Gradually, Jeff slowed the horses down to a regular walk.

"I....I have to think," he mumbled, letting his hands rest in his lap, holding the reins loosely. "I....I...can't believe it. I...." Jeff's mind had not quite grasped the full impact of what had just happened. His dreams were gone. He could not build his ranch. He didn't know what to do. "We...we might need to....to go back home....or... or... um, find a...another town...or..." His voice faded away and then he suddenly slapped his leg. "That should NOT have happened!!"

"You mean it wouldn't have happened if you hadn't had a woman with you?" Susannah said softly, looking forward at the horses' backs.

Jeff turned and looked at her, but she would not look back at him. He cleared his throat. "I....I didn't say that."

"Well, thank you," she said, reaching inside her collar, "For not letting him take me."

Susannah had pulled something out from under the high neckline of her dress as she talked. Now, she placed it in his lap. It was a wad of cash. He was so stunned, he actually jumped up. The money fell to the floor of the wagon and the reins jerked, stopping the horses.

"Susannah, what?! What on earth?"

He stooped to gather up all the bills, counting them as he went. Nearly all of his money was inexplicably sitting in his hands. He practically fell back onto his spot on the seat. Turning, he stared at her, wordless. His mouth hung open.

She was still staring away from him, her hands folded now, in her lap. "I hope he's satisfied with the three dollars I left in that pouch. It'll probably keep him busy at the saloon for at least a week. If he really thought there was more, he would've followed us by now. I bet he's wettin' his whistle as we speak, but I still think we oughtta get goin'. I wouldn't mind some distance between us and that town." She finally turned and looked at Jeff. He wouldn't know it, but the tears in her eyes were there because he had chosen her instead of the money. He had had no way of knowing that if he had made the other choice, he would have lost both. "When we put our purchases away, I saw him watching your pouch. I thought it might be prudent to not have all the money in it. So, I took most of it out and tucked it away without him seeing."

Jeff smiled. "You…uh…you thought it might be prudent…." He sighed, shaking his head in delighted consternation. "Thank you, Susannah. Thank you." He pushed the money into his pants pocket. "This is the entire loan my Pa gave me, plus my own savings. It's everything, Susie, for building my ranch, for buying my herd….I don't know what we would have done." He closed his eyes and then opened them. His voice was steady. "From now on, I'll keep this money spread in different hiding places, so, hopefully, no one can take all of it, and I'll put it in a bank near the ranch as soon as we get into the area….." He sighed again, looking into her eyes. "You saved everything, Susannah." She just stared back at him with nothing to say, just waiting and listening, filled with patience for his fumbling foolish ways. He was suddenly struck by her sweetness, her loveliness, just as he had been for a quick second when she had grabbed his hands during the wedding, before he had shaken away the sudden attraction. He did not hide from it this time. "You know," he whispered, "He was all wrong…." Very slowly, Jeff reached out and gently touched a tendril of hair that had escaped his wife's bun and slid down along her cheek. "All wrong….your hair's not like fire. It's more like a sunrise." She smiled at that and the transformation in her face, once again, made his heart skip a beat. He absolutely must make her smile more often. "Thank you, Susannah."

"You're welcome," she whispered back. Then she took the reins that had fallen and placed them into his hands, bringing him back to reality. Slowly he led the horses back around the town, keeping it far out of sight, and put their journey back on course.

***

Just before dusk, that night, Susannah and Jeff were feeling more at ease with each other than they had felt since their wedding day. Jeff took care of the horses and then spent several minutes hiding his money in four different hiding places in and on the wagon. While he worked, he observed Susannah as she boiled a little water in the one pot he owned, then stirred cornmeal and a little salt into it until it was mushy and partially cooked. Back home, a quiet Chinese man, that Jeff's Pa had hired long ago, did all the cooking behind the closed doors of the kitchen. On the trail with his grandfather every summer, he had been far too busy with the cattle to see the cook throw their simple fare together. So, all his life, Jeff had simply eaten whatever was put before him without knowing much about how his food was prepared. Observing Susannah plop the dodger batter onto a towel and then put beans into the same pot, Jeff admitted to himself that he found it very peaceful to watch her cook. She set the tin plate at the edge of the fire, with a few rocks beneath it to keep it level. Then she melted butter on it, waiting for it to sizzle as she stirred the beans. It was mesmerizing. He felt the tension of the day slipping away. His muscles relaxed and he sighed, approaching the fire and settling himself beside it. Susannah rolled heaping spoonfuls of the warm sticky cornmeal mixture between her fingers, deftly forming egg-shaped blobs and dropping them in the bubbling yellow liquid the butter had turned into.

"I suppose I should've thought of getting us some more dishes," Jeff mumbled, watching the corn dodgers growing golden and crispy. "At least another plate and cup for you, and you know, whatever you're supposed to be usin' to do whatever that is you're doin'."

"A skillet," she answered, in an amused voice. "Don't need none of that....We're makin' do just fine," Susannah said softly,

53

concentrating on turning the dodgers over, with her spoon, to fry the other sides.

"You really believe that, don't you?" Jeff said, cocking his head a little. "You just go with the flow, take what comes. I haven't heard you complain once." Susannah looked deliberately away from him and sprinkled some delicious-smelling herb over the beans. She did not answer him. "Look, Susie, I….," he took a breath, "I'm sorry that I thought you'd be like my mother. Clearly you're not, and while I'm willing to admit it was just plain stupid to think that all women were the same, that still doesn't mean that I want a wife," he folded his arms, trying to hold on to his determination. It had been inside him for so long. He couldn't let it go. "I guess, deep down, I always knew some women were perfectly nice….like….like you…,but I….just,…well,….I still just don't want a wife."

"I know," was all she said, but she looked up at him and their eyes locked and he suddenly felt like he could read her mind. He was saying he didn't want a wife and her eyes were saying, well, you've got one.

After a moment, she lowered her eyes and began scooping the crusty corn dodgers onto her towel. She used the edge of her apron to lift the hot plate and pour the last dregs of butter and all the steaming little crumbs into the beans. She hadn't wasted hardly any butter at all. She set the plate on the grass to let it cool and asked a question to change the mood, while she stirred the beans again.

"Jeffrey? Won't you tell me where we're headed?"

Jeff relaxed again, happy to talk about something else.

"We're headed up through the high plains to the southern edge of the sandhills. Good cattle grazing country up there."

"In Nebraska?" she asked. "That'll be nice."

"Why?" Jeff wondered, surprised at how much he wanted to know his wife's thoughts.

"Well, it's someplace new. A whole nother state," she said in her quiet voice, while spooning beans onto the still-warm tin plate. "What's it been? Two years? Since Nebraska became a state? I think it was '67. I've always loved hearin' about other places. Whenever Aunt Jane took me to the store, I'd always listen out for people talking about news." She suddenly paused and looked at him, a serene smile on her face. "Another state," she let out a slow satisfied sigh as she turned back to her work. "A whole new part of the country, so far from anywhere I've ever been."

"Yeah, I guess that's something we have in common," he responded, "A desire to get somewhere far away, somewhere fresh, somewhere where nobody knows us and we can hopefully be whatever we want to be."

Susannah decided it wouldn't be a good idea to mention how much she, once again, liked to hear him say "we". He claimed he didn't want a wife, but he seemed to be getting used to her, at least a little.

"We'll stop in Kearney for supplies and I want to check out the stock yards there," Jeff continued. "Then, we'll keep on pushing west until we get to North Platte. That's where we'll visit the land office and we can pick up anything else we might need. After that, it'll be wide open country until we find my ranch." Jeff's eyes took on a far away look. He was delighted to be talking about his dreams. He didn't want to acknowledge how nice it was to have someone to tell them to. "There's still a lot of unclaimed land left before you get to Ogallala," he said, waving his arm in the air as if pointing out across the sandhills they would see from his ranch. "As long as we stay south of the river, out of Sioux territory, we'll be just fine. I'm hoping for some nice sprawling grassland with maybe some woods not too far away." He smiled, thinking of the ranch he had always planned on building. "Cattle sales are booming since the war," he went on. "It's a great time to be a rancher, if I can just manage to get my herd goin' and growin'. It's gonna be a lot of work."

Susannah spoke softly, when Jeffrey had stopped talking and grown silent. His mind was at his future ranch. "You've been dreaming of it a long time, haven't you?" He nodded, still not looking at her, his thoughts hundreds of miles away, literally. "I've been dreaming a long time too."

"It's all that keeps us going sometimes, isn't it?" he responded, finally tilting his eyes towards her. "What do you dream about?"

As the question tumbled out of Jeff's mouth, unbidden, it surprised him. He was struck again by how interested he was in his wife. It had been developing gradually. He had not foreseen it. She was unwanted, he tried to remind himself, unnecessary, nothing but an extra hassle he didn't need, but in spite of all that, Jeffrey sure did like talking to her. That wasn't so bad, was it? If he had to have a wife, at least the one he'd gotten stuck with was interesting. His mind began to wander into other thoughts...interesting and kind....and patient...and a good cook....and hardworking....and stunningly beautiful. Suddenly, his jumbled unexpected thoughts were dispelled by Susannah's soft voice answering his question. He forced his mind to focus on what she was saying.

He had asked her what she dreamed about and she stopped moving for a moment to think of how to answer. "Well, nothing too big, nothing that should worry you. I've just always wanted to live in a quiet country place, away from towns and people. With, maybe, just a distant neighbor or two, hours away." She handed him the full plate and closed her eyes while he prayed for the food. Then, she continued, as she dipped water into their one tin mug. "And I've always wanted my own little kitchen with my own little garden outside---"

"That's right, you, uh...you mentioned that on our first day together, but I...well, I guess I wasn't listening so well that day." He looked at her, a quiet shame in his eyes that he wasn't yet ready to express in words.

"Yeah," Susannah continued quickly, not wanting him to dwell on the bad feelings of that first day, "I just want, you know, my very own quiet little world, where I can be left to my own devices, to plan and cook and grow things and sort of, you know…have my own ideas and try them out, without….uh…"

"Without anybody ordering you about, or forcing you to do things their way," he finished her thought for her.

She was startled. "How….how did you know that?"

"I think that's why I was always escaping to Grandpa's ranch, even after I started working at the bank." He sighed. "Actually, it was especially after that. That bank was my Pa's stuffy little empire, with him always barking commands and demanding that I have absolutely no thoughts of my own about how to run things. It was tedious and awful." He took a bite of beans, then passed the fork to her. "Grandpa's ranch was safe, even during the fighting. He lives down in western Texas. The war never got out that far. It was hard to get supplies during those years, and most of his cowboys headed east to join up, but I was too young to enlist, even if I'd known which side I wanted to be on, and he was too old, so we just kept on wrangling cattle. I loved learning about ranching, but I think what I loved more was not being ordered around, yelled at and forced to do things I wasn't interested in, you know, like the rest of the year." He took a sip of water. "I know it's not quite the same as the way the Kellys treated you, but still, I think I can understand a little."

"Yeah," Susannah nodded, swallowing a bite of her corn dodger, "We…both of us…we just want some freedom, I think. And I'm sorry, if being married makes you feel less free. I'll do my best not to be a hindrance to your plans."

"Yeah, well….," Jeff didn't know how to respond to that, "We'll see."

Chapter 7

The last three weeks of their journey went by quickly, as Susannah and Jeff were growing a little more comfortable with each other and no more giant mishaps occurred. After Jeff told her where they were going and what kind of land he was hoping to purchase, Susannah was delighted to have these new details to fill the long hours on the trail with daydreams of her changing life.

They spent a few hours in the thriving cattle town of Kearney. It was a clean bustling environment and Jeff felt that it was safe for the couple to have some space, each on their own. It was time to buy fresh supplies for their new home, so Jeff gave Susannah three dollars to buy dishes and headed off to survey the stockyards he hoped to use someday when he drove his cattle here. Susannah found good deals on used items traded at the store by settlers passing through. She bought a cheap clay mixing bowl, a skillet, a Dutch oven pot, a bread pan, a pie pan, a couple of baking sheets and a plate, cup, fork and spoon for herself. Then Jeff returned and, together, they stocked their wagon with flour and baking powder, spices, bacon, sugar, rice, jars for canning, seeds and a few other things. Jeff had already filled his small wagon with tools, and things he would need for building and other tasks, before he left home.

Six days later, they came to North Platte, a smaller town, but pleasant. Jeff went to the land office on his own, where he paid for a parcel of land that he chose from a map. Then he deposited what was left of his money in a nearby bank. While he did his business, Susannah took a dollar to a small nearby store to see if there was anything they might need that they had forgotten. She picked out a small mortar and pestle and a few sewing supplies. Then she wandered around the small room choosing another bag of cornmeal and a few other food items. She reveled again in the freedom of shopping on her own. She had never done so back in Seagleton and, on top of that, it was such an accomplishment that Jeffrey had let go of some of his intense desire to do everything his way, and on his own, and had begun to trust his new wife a little.

As Susannah paid for the items, the storekeeper said, "We still have a few war widows around these parts, if you've got any unattached men in your group...."

She wasn't used to being alone, without her cousins bouncing around, or her aunt nagging her to get things right. Talking to strangers brought a strange mix of delight and anxiety, but even in the buzz of newness, she wasn't careless enough to announce that she and Jeff were traveling alone. Being robbed once, was plenty. So, she just dipped her head, like the man's comment had embarrassed her, and gathered her purchases with a quick thank you.

The storekeeper's comment explained why she saw so many women walking up and down the wooden sidewalks and so few men. The war between the states had ended four years ago. Some towns were more touched than others by the events of the bloodiest time in their nation's history, so far. Susannah watched a woman walking alone with two small children and felt grateful, once again, to have a husband strong and whole, and grateful also that they could start their life unhaunted by the gruesome experiences so many carried with them. She tried to shake these grim thoughts away as she approached the wagon.

Jeff came out of the bank, grinning a little, eager to show her his new land on a map. Susannah was pleased to see the happy optimism in his eyes and wondered how long it might be before he thought of the ranch as she did, as not his land, but theirs, or if he ever would. After refilling their water, at a nearby stream, the couple, finally, set off on the last leg of their journey.

Susannah was very excited that her new home was only one more week away, in a virtually unsettled area of wild countryside. In the evenings, she stared at the map, and drank in Jeffrey's explanations as he pointed to a forest that would provide game right behind their house, a neighboring ranch nearly a day's ride away, an area of endless prairie, of which they now owned three hundred acres, and the mighty river Platte just five miles north of them, marking the beginning of Sioux territory. It was all so beautiful to her, more than just lines on a map, but a whole bright future filled with potential. It sat there west of them, like an unturned page of a book, waiting to be seen.

A few days later, as they turned off a well-used road and headed into unsettled land, the wagon began to tilt, startling both Jeff and his wife. Susannah had never experienced the front of the wagon being higher than the back. Her body was being pushed backwards against her will. She grabbed, instinctively, for the side of the wagon, gripping tightly as the auburn bun at the nape of her neck was forced back against the wagontop's canvas behind her. Her feet came off the floor. She gasped, but before she could say anything about this strange phenomenon, the horses found the top of the incline and the wagon righted itself, jolting the newlyweds forward again and slamming their feet back into the floorboards. Still, they couldn't say a word, because their breath had been taken away by the sudden appearance of a vast new landscape, spreading out before them, so far that the edges were beyond their visions' ability to absorb.

Susannah's eyes widened in surprise at the sight of a limitless grassland, going on and on to the horizon, but it was not the same green as the simple plains of Kansas. It was more of a soothing golden, like wheat on a sunny afternoon, glinting and sparkling in the distant breezes, so perfectly fresh and lovely, but it wasn't the color that shocked her the most. Susannah had never been out of Kansas in her whole life, and Kansas was flatter than a pancake under an anvil. Her brain knew the world this way, stretching out in every direction totally uniform, always. Nebraska was so different. What lay below her was the edge of the sandhills, reaching to the north as far as the eye could see. The ground rippled like a sheet undulating in the wind. It moved up and down in a strange beautiful pattern, rolling and sloping unpredictably. Their wagon sat at the top of Susannah's first hill and for the very first time, she looked down and saw an endless land below. It was extremely exciting for someone who had never looked anywhere but around, or forward, examining only flatness. Looking down and outward was like being in another world. The hills were small, like a choppy brook's surface, all flowing left and right and into the distance, staying low and soft, with light grass growing over the sandy uneven ground.

Jeffrey smiled, taking in this wonderful place. The terrain wasn't so unknown to him. Having traveled back and forth to Texas, and seen everything in between, Jeff had experienced many types of countryside, but this was different. This was going to be his home. Somewhere, two or three days travel into those wild waving knolls, lay his ranch. He could already see the cattle, in his mind's eye, spattered across the grassy slopes, like brushstrokes on a painting. He was experiencing a moment of pure joy, his first in a long time. It wasn't just the stunning vista below, or the prospect of his longed-for future lost ahead in those grassy hills somewhere, waiting to be found, that made him feel a burst of hope and happiness. It was the combination of all that, along with the glistening pleasure in Susannah's eyes. Her mouth hung open in awe and her face shined with sheer bliss. It tore his gaze away from the view. He couldn't stop looking at his wife. He had never seen anything so beautiful as her face, radiant with discovery and pleasure. He wanted to see her that way more and more and more. He knew he would never grow tired of it.

Suddenly overwhelmed with confusion, Jeff shook the warm feelings away. This was the problem with having a woman in your life, he told himself. You can get drawn in by her beauty, or how good it feels when she's happy, and forget how hard it is to always be looking out for her and having to consider her as a part of your decisions. It was just as Susannah had said, a loss of freedom, and he had not signed up for it. Well, he rebuked himself inwardly, he sort of *had* signed up for it, but he had not really meant to. Marriage had never been what he wanted and he didn't like the way he kept forgetting that. He wasn't used to being confused or swinging back and forth on how he felt or what he wanted. He did not like it one bit. He abruptly felt annoyed, and slapped the reigns, pulling the wagon roughly down into the sandhills, without saying anything about the milestone he and Susannah had just experienced looking at their new world for the first time.

Jeff seemed irritated into the evening and all through the next day, but Susannah just ignored it. She was no longer afraid of his bluster and she was too caught up in her own glee. Being in this new place, so close to her new life, where all her dreams would be fulfilled, was overwhelming. Joy and anticipation was all she could think of, and it took all her strength to remain calm and not annoy Jeff further, who clearly did not feel the same, at first. Thankfully, over time, he settled down and began to relax, as they drew closer and closer to his dreams too.

There was another property before they reached their own. The government worker at the land office had told them that this small ranch was owned by the Anderson family and they would be the Bridges' only neighbors. Jeff's three hundred acres was a day's travel past the Anderson Ranch. Three days after entering the sandhills, the newlyweds finally reached their neighbors' land. They were eager to meet them.

Chris Anderson and his cheerful wife, Ashley, were a

middle-aged couple living in a fine three bedroom house with their teenage son and two younger daughters. They were absolutely delighted to meet their new neighbors. The friendly pair embraced Jeff and Susannah and welcomed them wholeheartedly, insisting that they have a big breakfast together. Susannah and Ashley whipped up fried eggs and flapjacks to go with the bacon and molasses that Susannah contributed. The kids brought a pail of fresh milk and a jar of mulberry jam in from the barn to add to the sumptuous fare and everyone sat down at the Andersons' rough-hewn table for a hardy happy meal and good conversation. They all talked excitedly about the sandhills, ranch life and starting out from scratch on a new piece of land. The Andersons imparted many stories of the time they were in the Bridges shoes, building their new home, nearly twenty years ago.

After washing the dishes, the two women went out to admire Ashley's kitchen garden. The young girls hung around, ecstatic to have visitors at their isolated home, while Susannah plied Ashley with questions about gardening in this part of the country. Jeffrey checked out Chris' barn, corrals and bunkhouse. He spoke to the Andersons' two ranch hands, and soaked up Chris' advice about starting a ranch and caring for a herd.

It was a pleasant visit, but Jeff was chomping at the bit to get to his new land, which was only a day's travel away. The older couple understood how anxious the Bridges were to get to their land. They had been that way once, not so long ago. So, after just three hours at the Anderson Ranch, Jeff insisted that they get going. The youngest Anderson girl, 8-year-old Elinor, handed Susannah a picked wildflower as she climbed into the wagon. Susie thanked her with a smile and tucked the pale purple coneflower behind her ear.

Chris shook Jeff's hand with a firm grip and said, "You just remember to call on us when you get to buildin' bigger things like the barn and the bunkhouse. I know it's down the road a ways, but you'll be needin' more than a few sets of hands for some jobs. My boy and I will be happy to help, and you can return the favor the next time a big job needs doin' around here."

Jeff nodded and thanked the kind-hearted man, then climbed up beside Susannah, touched his hat towards Mrs. Anderson and her daughters, then shook the reins and rolled slowly out of the pretty little farmyard. Chickens scattered, ranch hands waved and cattle mooed in the distance. A shiver ran up Susie's spine as she had a sudden thought that this moment was a premonition of what her life would be like. She wrapped her arms around herself, momentarily overpowered with joyful anticipation. She had never wanted anything so much in her life as she did this new home ahead, and she felt like she might just fly apart if she had to wait another minute. It was a good waiting, though, she reminded herself, calming down, and it wouldn't be much longer now.

Chapter 8

After an hour, the newlyweds had passed all of the fences of the modest Anderson Ranch and headed back into open country. Jeff was telling Susannah how his ranch would be the same size as their neighbors, in the beginning, but he planned to expand as the years went by. After the war between the states had ended, the east had developed a taste for beef, and cattle ranching was growing rapidly now. Jeff was hopeful that the popularity and profit of the industry would continue, and make his life's work a huge success. Susannah enjoyed listening to him talk about his plans as the rest of the day went by.

After spending the night in a small copse of trees, they continued heading west and, just as dawn was breaking, they came across a large rock with a pointed tip at the peak of a big hill. This was the boundary marker the land office had registered as the beginning of the acreage that Jeffrey had bought. Shaking, and grinning with expectation, Jeff jumped down from the wagon, barely remembering to set the break, and ran, full speed, to the crest of the hill. Susannah followed eagerly, and the two of them gasped at the sight below them.

A delicate orange sunrise was blooming over a rich green forest below them where the outer fringe of the Platte valley faded into the endless golden plains. The last of the tall, breeze-swaying trees, gave way to miles of wide open prairie rippled with gentle grass-covered slopes. A smoky gray peregrine falcon swooped out of the woods, scooped up a young vole and disappeared back into the grove it came from, disturbing a group of bright yellow meadowlarks pecking for seeds in the brush. The faint shimmer of a pale blue stream was visible to the west, sneaking quietly from the cover of the woods and cutting a clean line across the Bridges' new land, whispering of baths, spic-and-span dishes, fresh laundry and plenty to drink. A nearly invisible hare hopped in and out of grasses that matched its color, making a bee-line for the water. The sparkling sun spilled more and more rays of warm pink, and deep purple, and searing white, as it rose, dappling the untouched land with rolling light. The area that Jeffrey had selected was a stunning masterpiece of color and life. It was clean and unscarred, moving with wildlife, growing things and endless potential. Susannah had never seen anything so perfectly lovely.

Jeffrey was more excited than he had ever felt before. It was bursting out of him. He wanted to do something, something physical. He couldn't quite bring himself to jump up and down like a little boy would, but his arms and legs were practically buzzing with energy. Susannah had just appeared at his side, her face filled with a huge grin. He turned to her, impulsively, took ahold of her waist and twirled the both of them round and round.

"It's my ranch," he yelled at the top of his lungs. "Susannah, it's my ranch! I made it!"

"Yes, you did!" Susannah was giggling uncontrollably. "You made it! We made it! It's your ranch and it's beautiful!"

She was too happy for her new husband, seeing the sheer elation pouring out him, and too happy for herself too, to care that he had not included her in his emotional claim of this place. A small part of her wanted to say 'our ranch', but she kept quiet. Hopefully, someday he would say it on his own and it would mean more.

Susannah felt genuinely thrilled for Jeffrey. She had not expected that. Her new husband's success and joy had come to mean a lot to her and she didn't mind the feeling. She enjoyed it, and the fact that his accomplishment meant that she would get the life she wanted too, made the moment so giddy that she almost felt lightheaded. She gazed out and out and out at the boundless beauty of her new home and was overcome by it all. Without thinking, she reached out and hugged Jeffrey. It was their first embrace. She hoped it would not be the only one they would ever have. Susannah startled herself, and felt suddenly nervous over what she was doing, but she did not let go. To her surprise Jeff responded reflexively, by wrapping his arms tight around her. His hug was warm and sweet, and he rocked her gently back and forth. She closed her eyes in pure contentment.

***

The first thing they did after coming down from the big hill, was drive along the southern edge of their woods until they reached the stream. For a moment, the couple stared around at the trees and insect-tickled weeds, listening to the wind rustling the branches and the skitters of small animals. They imagined the twenty acres of forest they owned, spreading further than they could see, shielding them from the travelers' trails that ran along the shallow Platte River just a few miles north of them. The forest would provide for plenty of hunting and foraging as it extended far further than their own acreage. The river nearby provided a respite from the arid conditions of the sandy Nebraskan plains, creating a perfect oasis of greenery and moisture in its rich river valley. Susannah couldn't get over the amazing contrast between the lush green thickets to north and the vast open prairie to the south. The way the two polar opposite landscapes rushed together and met in the middle, peacefully intertwining along their cozy border, like two friends coming together after a long absence. Jeffrey had chosen well where to put down his roots and build his dream ranch. Susannah resolved that she must do everything she could to help them both have a productive successful life here.

Jeff wandered around for a long time, joyfully picking the ideal spot for his farmyard, the place which would eventually be the center of his little world, the headquarters of his ranch. He hoped someday it would be a bustling hub of activity, with not only a grand house, but a huge barn, a bunkhouse, different kinds of corrals and his very own ranch hands running around, engaged in various tasks, and calling him "Boss".

Jeff surveyed the area from different spots and angles, standing with his hands on his hips, turning in every direction, and bending down to feel the earth. Susannah strolled along the edge of the forest, picking a few herbs, but mostly just watching her husband quietly, fascinated by his exhaustive examination of their new home and waiting patiently for him to choose the spot for their cabin.

"We'll build it here," Jeff finally proclaimed, jogging up to Susannah. He was pointing to a spot shaded by the woods and nestled in a crook of the stream. "It's close to the water and the trees, and the ground is good and solid here. It will face outward across the cattlefields…" He waved his arm, indicating each area he mentioned. His voice trailed off as his eyes saw what would someday be here.

"It's perfect," Susannah said softly, smiling brightly and slipping her arm through his.

He tore his gaze away from his imaginings and reveled in his wife's approval and delight. Looking at her, he wondered what it would have been like to have no one to tell of his plans, to be here all alone, making these huge decisions, with no one to share them with.

***

Over the next few days, a lot of work was done. Jeff had a makeshift corral, made out of rope and branches, built for the horses by the end of the first day. Susannah paced off the space for the kitchen garden just fifteen feet from the stream. She staked it at the four corners. Jeff did the same for the cabin ten feet to the right of the garden. He talked of finding rocks for a fireplace and the need to build a table and chairs. He spoke of putting shelves and pegs on the walls. Susannah just listened quietly, not mentioning the need for a bed, or a seating area near the fire, or practical things like windows and doors. Jeff would get around to it all eventually.

As the rest of the week went by, Jeffrey insisted that he would do all the work on the cabin by himself just as he had always planned to do. He said his grandfather had taught him how to build and made him construct a shed, all on his own, at the age of thirteen. He said he did not need any help and building a cabin was not women's work. Though Susannah knew little of building, she knew things would go more efficiently with her assistance, but for a while she contented herself with laundry, cooking, preparing the ground for the inside of the cabin, organizing the belongings that were unloaded from the wagon, so Jeff could take it to carry rocks, and getting the garden started before the rest of spring was lost.

Although Susannah loved every minute of the work she was doing to start this new life she'd always dreamed of, she was biding her time, waiting for the right moment to insert herself into Jeffrey's process. She would show him that he did need her. Sure, he could build a cabin on his own, but it would be extra hard, more dangerous and take far longer than it would with another set of hands. Susannah did not believe that her husband's stubbornness was a good enough reason for him to risk injury, or delay their move into their house. She had never really been stubborn herself, but she was growing and trying new things, and she felt much braver about disagreeing with Jeff than she had in the early days. She would try a little of her own hardheadedness to match his, and see what happened.

For days Susannah waited, until Jeffrey had chopped down all the logs, dragged them out of the depth of the forest with the horses' help, and trimmed, notched and prepared them. She watched patiently as he spent a day and a half building a stone fireplace and chimney, then moved on to carefully laying the first two logs on each wall. Now, the task would get harder as he lifted each log higher and higher, attempting to secure one end and then the other somehow. Now was the time for her to jump in. She said a little prayer, asking that Jeff would accept her help and not be mad. Afterall, this was the part where two sets of hands would be needed the most. Surely, he could see that. He had to, and Susannah wanted so much to help build her own home.

Wearing the worn garden gloves that had traveled with her in her carpet bag, she walked directly over to where Jeffrey was lifting one end of a heavy log, trying to leverage it onto the two logs that made up the bottom of the cabin's western wall. He was managing fine, but the next log and the one after that would not be so easy. Susannah bent down, without a word, and picked up the other end of the log, surprising herself that she'd been able to move it on the first try. Feeling the weight of the log shift, Jeff was startled. His eyes swung to Susannah's end.

"What are you doing?!" he exclaimed, dropping the log. It bounced and rolled. Susannah hopped back, just barely getting her toes out of the way, but she did not get upset. She had expected Jeff to react this way. Immediately, Susannah reached out and stopped the log from rolling into her garden.

She gave a little sigh. "Jeff, let me help you." She did not look at him.

"No! Absolutely not! I told you I'm going to do this myself like I've always planned. I don't need help." He picked up his end of the log again, braced his feet and began scooting backwards towards the wall again, pulling the log. Susannah waited while he grunted and dragged the heavy log halfway up onto the other log. He then headed towards her end, but she stood in his way. He stopped and stared at her.

"Why, Jeff? Why can't you change your plans?" she said softly, reaching out and gently putting her hand on his shoulder. Her meekness and gentle touch stopped him in his tracks. He glared, trying to form an answer, but couldn't. So, Susannah continued. "You don't have to *need* help to accept some. I *know* you can do it on your own. *You* know you can, but you don't have to. You've got me to help, and if we do it together you might be able to get your herd before winter." He folded his arms and turned away from her. He really *did* want to get his first herd as soon as he could, but he clung to his stubbornness, staring out across the stream. "Jeff, it's nearly summer and we still have a barn to build and miles of fences, not to mention all the little things. If I help with the cabin, we can get to everything at least a week or two faster, I think. It could make the difference between whether you get your herd this year or have to wait 'til next year. Please, let me help. It's what I'm here for."

"What do you mean?" He finally turned to look at her.

"It's a wife's place to help her husband any way she can, right?" She tilted her head a little, looking at him calmly. "Please, I want to help. It's my home too."

"I never wanted a wife to help or otherwise and…and…I never wanted this to be your home too!" Jeff's voice was raising. "This was supposed to me my home and mine alone." His chest heaved a little with the strength of his outburst. An outburst that he immediately regretted the second he saw the hurt look on Susannah's face.

They stared at each other for a moment, then Susannah got a strange look in her eye. "No…," she said slowly, shaking her head, "That's not it at all, is it?" Realization was filling her face and she smiled a little. "I've been getting to know you for over a month now, Jeff, and I think there is more to this." She put her hands on her hips. "You don't think I can do it, do you? And…and," she tilted her head again, leaning closer to him and giving him a little good-natured shove, "And you.. think I'm going to get hurt. You're actually a little worried about me. Admit it."

"I…I will not!" Jeff said. She had shocked him, reading his mind like that, and revealing thoughts he didn't realize he had until she voiced them.

"Well, I've got news for you, Jeffrey Bridges," Susannah smiled even bigger, "You still have a lot to learn about women. I'm not fragile and I've got powerful muscles."

Jeff's bad mood vanished in an uncontrollable laugh at his wife's hilarious comment. He had not laughed like that since he was a child.

More determined than ever now, Susannah kept talking as she aggressively rolled up each sleeve past the elbow. "For ten years these arms have cleaned and sewed and cooked and weeded." She ignored her husband's mirth, tightening her gloves. "They've mended fences, hitched up wagons, carried babies and scrubbed laundry for a family of eight. Believe me, these arms are stronger than you think." With that she bent down, picked up her end of the log, and swung it up onto the knee-high one beside her. Jeffrey's mouth hung open in shock and all he could do was pick up the wooden mallet nearby and hammer the new log down into the notches before his wife suggested that she do it herself.

Chapter 9

After a long day of lifting logs together and hammering them into place, Jeffrey had to admit they had accomplished nearly twice as much as he could have done on his own. He came back from his evening chores to find Susannah sitting by the fire, stirring their supper. He could see the evidence of all the work she had done to fix them just one meal. The new Dutch oven pot was on its side buried in coals nearby, most likely baking a pie. He could see the now empty fruit jar sitting nearby, next to bags of sugar and flour. A piece of flat wood had a towel over it. The towel held a freshly sliced loaf of bread baked that morning. A block of butter sat next to it in a bowl. Looking in their refuse bucket, Jeff found the leftover parts of an unidentifiable small animal carcass, along with a few discarded bits of potatoes and onions. Susannah had not only prepped vegetables from their recent purchases and made a pie, but also checked the snares he had set at the edge of the woods, cleaned and butchered what she found and was now stirring a thick hearty stew to replenish all the energy they had lost from their day of intense physical effort. Jeff could no longer deny that having Susannah around had its benefits. He never could have kept himself so well fed. Such things were important, he now realized. They needed to stay strong for their busy life, especially at this early stage of hard labor. Susannah knew that, and she just did whatever needed doing without ever saying a word about it.

As he approached, he watched her stretching her neck back and forth. While one hand stirred with a much-too-small spoon, her other hand reached up to work a kink out of her shoulder. Jeff wanted so much to touch her, to help her with the aches the day had brought. Never in his life had he thought of such a thing. Never before had his hands reached out, without him telling them to, as they were doing now. He hesitated, when his fingers had almost reached her collar and stared at his hands, frozen in mid-air, but his desire to ease Susannah's pain and feel her skin beneath his hands, overpowered his qualms. She was his wife, he told himself. There was nothing wrong with rubbing away the tension from her shoulders.

"Here, let me help….," he said, quietly, settling his hands against the cloth beneath them, feeling the warmth of her body through the fabric. He let them rest there, waiting for her reaction. Would she pull away?

She tensed up at first, surprised, uncomfortable, but the same thoughts that had run through Jeff's mind, entered Susannah's as well. He was her husband. Surely it was ok to let him massage away the ache from her neck. It might be nice. So, she relaxed, setting the spoon aside and resting her hands in her lap.

Seeing that Susannah was agreeable, Jeff began to knead her shoulders with a rhythmic motion. She let out a little sigh of pleasure and her shoulders relaxed even more. He moved his hands up to her neck, feeling her smooth skin and massaging it in small circles. Ripples of a strange tingling sensation were running up his arms. He liked this. He liked it too much. Her hair was so rich and glowing in the firelight. Her smell intoxicated him with the heady scent of sweat and wood and some indefinable womanly quality. He would have been happy to do this every single day.

Susannah closed her eyes in mellow delight. She had never felt anything like this. It was wonderful. She liked the way Jeff faltered at first, his hands moving slowly for a while and then picking up momentum. She was surprised at how much she had grown to want his touch without even knowing it. She knew she would be longing for it even more after this. She began to feel a sharp connection with Jeff, a bridge was slowly being built between them, board by board and step by step. This moment could be a turning point. She knew that on some level, but her mind was too fluid right now to notice. His hands were moving to her skin, caressing the hairs beneath her bun. The pins were loosening. Warmth began to run through her like a strong blush. She had never experienced such sensations.

Jeff was beginning to feel overwhelmed. He had to stop. He didn't know where he was going, what he was doing. He needed solid ground. So, he cleared his throat and spoke. His voice broke the spell.

"Um...I'm sorry you're uh....feeling sore." He moved to sit beside her. "I knew that would happen."

Susannah shook herself. The absence of his touch struck her oddly. It was a worse feeling that the aches in her muscles. She shivered, the way one does when something has unsettled them, but she covered it by reaching for the spoon and returning to her work.

"Aches and pains are ok," she mumbled, finding her mental footing again with effort. "It just means that I've been working. I like work, when it's my choice. Work gets things done, creates things. Work is life."

She reached out and spread a fresh cloth over Jeff's lap and then proceeded to put a piece of buttered bread on it.

"Yeah," Jeff replied, accepting the bowl of stew she was handing him. "I feel the same way. Never met a woman that felt that way though."

"I think you haven't met many women or really gotten to know any....maybe? Jeff?" She wondered out loud as she scooped her own stew.

"That's fair....," Jeff answered quietly. "It's....yeah....it's true."

Things grew very quiet, as Jeff led them in prayer for the food, and remained quiet for several minutes as the sun slowly set and the fire crackled. Many thoughts were spinning in Jeff's mind, worries and upsets that had been battling there for weeks. It was time he spoke of them.

"Susie, I'm sorry for….for earlier…," Jeff stared into the flames, too ashamed to look at his wife.

Susannah was surprised. "For what?"

"For what I said,…you know…about not wantin'….this… to be your …home…" The words slid out gradually. It was hard for him to be apologetic. He was not used to it. He acknowledged in his heart that that was definitely a flaw to be worked on. "I think we both knew that that's how I feel, but to say it out loud like that….again…it was hurtful and I ….I don't really ever….mean… to be hurtful." He finally forced himself to look at her. "Really, Susannah, I…I don't."

Ever the comforter, Susie reached out reflexively and took his hand. He stared down at it, surprised at how good it felt for his fingers to be held by hers. Six weeks ago, he would never have guessed that such a thing would ever be pleasant.

"I know you don't, Jeffrey," she whispered, letting him off the hook in her usual forgiving way. It made him feel worse. "It's ok."

"It's not ok," he put down his stew and turned to her, ready to be a man about this. He folded his other hand over hers. "The truth is, Susannah, an apology is long overdue." He watched as her brows came together in confusion. She really wasn't holding a grudge at all about the hard moments that had been running around and around in his brain for weeks. She had let them go long ago, but he couldn't. "I'm sorry for the way I treated you on that first day."

Susannah sighed calmly, her free hand coming up to gently rub his arm in reassurance. "Jeffrey, you already apologized in a lot of little ways,… like, when we were in that dangerous town and… and after…"

"That's not good enough," Jeffrey squeezed her hand tighter. "I was cruel to you, Susannah-- snapping at you, so angrily.... It must have frightened you to think you had married a man with a temper. I'm sorry if I made you afraid of me, and for the way I said you'd better not ever be a bother, it was so insulting and it's kind of been haunting me." He blinked and gulped in a deep breath of air. "I...I'm ashamed,... Susie... and...and you didn't deserve that....and....and it wasn't really like me—"

"I've learned what your really like," Susannah interrupted. "That day was just a very bad day for you, your lifelong dreams were slipping away. Being mad was understandable, and it's clear that you've learned that you didn't like yourself that way and well, ... that's what we do, we learn and grow and change. I've changed a lot since I met you too."

"I don't think you need to change, Susannah, but I certainly do." He closed his eyes and his voice fell to a whisper. "The way I spoke to you that day.....It was inexcusable...I'm so sorry, Susie, and it shouldn't have taken me so long to say it."

"It's all right," she reached out and ran her fingers along the side of his face making him open his eyes and look at her. "I forgive you."

Involuntarily, Jeff's whole body relaxed. Things he couldn't label were released inside him, like birds slipping from their fetters. Words of forgiveness were like magic, especially from Susannah's lips. Such powerful words and so gentle at the same time. It was a feeling he had never experienced before. There had been a lot of that since he had met her. He sighed slowly. Looking into Susannah's calm unselfish eyes as she spoke such kindness to him, Jeff felt so many brand new things all at once,-- relieved, at peace, cared about,-- he suddenly wanted to hold her, but he resisted such an odd unfamiliar wish. "Thank you," he said softly, moving his top hand to cover her slim fingers where they had fallen back to his forearm. He liked the feeling of her hands resting on him. "I've decided I'm going to make the best of this situation. It's like you say, we have to take what comes with dignity, and just persevere and …. I …I think that's the kind of man I want to be."

"I think the man you are is just fine, Jeffrey." She pulled her hands free, reached for his bowl and handed it to him. "We're going to be ok."

Jeff breathed deeply as the moment faded and they began to eat. He knew Susannah was trying to show him, every day, that having a wife wasn't so bad, and, in spite of himself, he was learning the lesson. It wasn't so bad at all.

Chapter 10

Before Susannah could blink, the spring was gone and the summer was flying past. A roof of heavy bark had been added to their cabin and Joshua had fashioned a table, stump stools and a bed. He built a stronger corral for the horses, a sturdy fence around the kitchen garden, and invited the Andersons and their ranch hands to help put up a barn. The barn raising was wonderful fun. Susannah had never spent such lovely time with friends before.

By mid-July, Susannah and Jeffrey had the beginnings of a thriving ranch. Jeffrey believed that the small herd he wanted to start out with soon, would be safer with a fence around the property. It was hard for a small operation to maintain a healthy herd using the open range. They would not be able to afford to lose any cattle when their numbers were so low. Also, Jeff explained to Susie, open range ranching could often be rife with violent disputes and expensive conflicts between ranchers. Jeff didn't feel that he knew enough yet about the business itself, or about the character of other ranchers of the region, to take the risk. So, he became very determined to build a strong fence around his entire acreage. It was hard work and time consuming. He spent most of his days far away from the cabin, gathering wood for the fence, or out putting up the fence, leaving Susannah alone to do her own work. She packed him dinner every morning, put it in his saddlebag and watched him ride off. He came home in the late afternoons, dirty and exhausted, but filled with stories of minor mishaps and interesting wildlife, and surprisingly eager to hear what accomplishments Susannah had made in his absence. The couple grew to cherish the evening time when they relaxed at the table over whatever sumptuous culinary creations Susannah always managed to conjure up, and talked and smiled together. Then they'd fall into sleep, always with Jeffrey pressing himself against the wall, and with Susannah too tired to wonder anymore if he was ever going to let himself hold her.

So, for months, life was good, in Susannah's opinion. It was a better life than any she had ever lived. It was exactly what she had dreamed of, since she was an unhappy child who had just moved into her aunt and uncle's cold uncomfortable house. Once a person has endured a tragic loss, or spent years being treated poorly, they have nothing to complain about when given a peaceful life in a beautiful place with freedom and purpose. She was very happy to work hard to build a home. It's something she'd always wanted to do.

The western side of the cabin became known as the kitchen, where Susannah had shelves and pegs for all her cooking tools and dishes. She kept jars of various things there, and washed dishes in a little basin under the window. The basin sat on a shelf that was about waist high. Sometimes, in those first few weeks, Susannah would catch herself thinking of something she needed and telling herself it was 'in the kitchen'. Then her hands would fly to her face in joy, as she thought, 'my kitchen, with the window that shines out to my garden'. It was everything she had always wanted. Once in a while, she even allowed herself the indulgence of dreaming of more, of one day having sweet children of her very own, if Jeff ever wanted to produce children with her. She longed for a little girl learning to wash dishes at her side, while a little boy practiced his first riding lesson out in the corral, with his Pa holding him in front as they rode together. She would look down at her tiny daughter and tell her that soon she would be riding too. Susannah's new dreams were happy things and her days were filled with peace.

She found a fresh joy in the same domestic tasks she'd been doing for years. Somehow, every chore felt different now, than it had felt back at her aunt and uncle's house, because every chore was her own. Susie did everything however she wanted to do it, which was something she had never experienced. Susannah relished the newness of that feeling. She felt like the queen of her own little kingdom and was perfectly content to fill her days with the hard work of gardening, cooking, laundry, cleaning, sewing and dozens of other lovely fulfilling responsibilities, and to reap the benefits of each. She found purpose in, not only her own satisfactions and needs fulfilled, but in watching the ranch grow and in seeing the subtle effects of her efforts on her husband's demeanor. The way he smiled or grew comfortable with certain routines, or said thank you or gave compliments, it sometimes felt like all she could ever want. Susannah was very happy.

No one ordered her around anymore and she did not miss that at all. Almost everything was her choice, her way, her home, not someone else's. Jeffrey didn't mind letting her run the house and garden her own way and he never interfered. That was exactly as she had dreamed. Against his will, Jeff had given Susannah everything she ever wanted, and she only wished that she could give him something in return. There were things she began to realize that she longed to give him, but he didn't want her in that way. Would he ever? Could she stand that loss, if he never did? He pulled away from her at night, and even in the day, if she opened her arms to hug him. It seemed so strange to her. She knew little of such things, but it seemed to her that a man should surely want a women who was ready and willing and totally his. It was the only source of sorrow in her mostly wonderful life, but when she felt such things it made her feel ungrateful, so she brushed them away and focused on the things she liked about her husband. She was fond of the way he called her 'Susie'. She had only ever been called, 'Susie', in kindness, from Elsie and the kids and her parents long ago. Aunt Jane had always said, 'Susannah', sternly, like it had an exclamation point permanently burned at the end of it, and Uncle Byron had almost always called her, 'Sue', if he used a name for her at all. It was like he couldn't be bothered with the few extra seconds it would have taken to say 'Susannah'. Sometimes she was sure he said it because he truly couldn't even remember her whole name. Jeff was not like that. He always took the time to call her 'Susie' or 'Susannah', in his rich strong tones, and to look at her when he spoke. She had grown to love the sound of his voice. She still had a lot to learn about him, but he was mostly polite, sometimes kind, and, once in a while, she thought she felt genuine warmth from him. Susannah had nothing but hope for a better and better future between them, if she just had the patience to wait for it, and if there was one thing she was good at, it was patience.

So, for several weeks, in Susannah's mind, the future looked bright and life seemed almost perfect, but life never remains that way. Soon, Susie began to feel doubts and worries and the light of her happy world grew slowly dimmer.

Jeff usually had one or more of the horses with him during the day and Susannah would go out to the barnyard to greet her husband and his horse when they returned for the evening. She loved horses and would pet their noses and talk to them. Occasionally, if there wasn't something that needed close attention in the kitchen, she would be the one to brush down the large docile animals, instead of Jeff, and lock them in their stalls in the brand new barn.

One afternoon, Susannah watched through the window as she washed the first carrots from her garden. She was very excited to be finally eating her own produce, from her own garden, just as she had always dreamed. She couldn't wait to show Jeffrey. Setting the carrots aside, she headed for the fireplace, turned tonight's meat on its spit near the edge, and removed from the hot stone hearth a pod of ruby red sumac berries she had found blooming a little early on the plentiful plains around the cabin. Feeling that they were perfectly dry now, she pulled off a handful of the tiny tart balls and dropped them into a pot of simmering water that was almost boiling over the fire. Then she headed back to the table and crushed the rest of the berries with her small mortar and pestle. The resulting flavorful dust would taste lovely sprinkled over her carrots, after she infused them with more of the sumac essence that was already steeping in the water.

Susannah smiled as she began to chop the carrots. A breeze blew onto her face through the glass-free window, as she stared peacefully outward across the ranch. Their two quarter horses were different colors. The one resting in the corral today was the deep brown Merriment, who had apparently been extremely frisky and fun in her youth when she had been named. The lighter colored one Jeff was walking in now. Susie was happy to catch sight of them both. The tired horse was named Duckling, because of her fuzzy blonde mane and silky yellowish hide. As, Susie's hands scrubbed the dirt from one more of her beloved carrots, her eyes took in Duckling's sweaty sides and puffing breath. Jeff had told his wife, that morning, that he had waited too long to survey the vicinity more fully, and though he felt it was important to know more about the area he lived in, he did not want to lose much work time exploring. So, he had planned to ride the horse hard today and canvass the length of the ranch's borders, cross some of the nearby ridges and hillocks to see what was beyond his sightlines from the edges of his land, and then travel around the woods all the way to the river and around the other side of the forest to return home. Clearly, he had done as he planned and covered a lot of ground, for both he and the horse looked exhausted. The water was lightly boiling now and Susannah watched the red dots of sumac churning around happily as she dropped the chopped carrots in to cook. Then, Susie headed out to greet her husband and his faithful mount. As she approached, a raw carrot in her hand, she saw Jeff gently pulling Duckling's head away from the water before she drank too much. It was better for a hot horse to drink in small snatches with cool-down time in between.

Jeff put his arms around the quarter horse's neck and rubbed her mane. "That's a good horse, Ducky." He patted her, his cheek against her strong side. "A good ride today, my girl. Let's get you into a cool stall, now." He gently led the horse into the barn, picking up Merriment on the way. Susannah followed, tucking the carrot into the back of her apron. It would be easier for Duckling to digest food once she had cooled down a little.

"We've got our first carrots today, Jeff," Susannah said softly.

Jeffrey closed and latched the second stall door, one hand still patting Duckling's nose across the waist high wood. "Really?" His eyes lit up as he looked at his wife. "The firstfruits of our labors, so to speak. The very first food to grow on our land." He smiled big. "Yep. A man sure likes to hear that." He patted his wife on the shoulder. "Good job, Susannah. That garden has always looked so neat and healthy. I can't wait to taste your carrots."

Susannah smiled back. "They'll take a while to boil and soften, so I'll give Ducky her rub-down."

"Oh, well, ok then," Jeff said, stepping away. "I reckon it'll be good to spend a few extra minutes washin' up after my other chores. I smell more like dirt and sweat and horse than usual tonight."

Susannah snickered at her husband's comment as he left the barn. Then she turned toward the golden horse and scratched her behind the ears. "You worked hard today didn't you, Ducky-girl?" She opened the stall and stepped inside. "A nice rub-down is going to feel so good, right?"

Susannah took a curry comb down from its peg nearby. Her father and uncle had always used a rag, and Jeffrey had had to show her how to use this new-fangled tool, but she had quickly grown used to the relatively new invention. She used it now to knock dirt, loose hair and other debris from Duckling's hide, soothing the horse as she went. Then she followed the combing with a bucket of cool water poured slowly over the horse's back and then brushed away with a soft brush. She slid the brush over Duckling's body, following the grain and smoothing the horse's creamy shining hair. She felt the horse's muscles relax beneath her gentle touch and watched as Duckling's breathing slowed back to its normal rhythm. The horse was beginning to cool down and was ready for another drink. Susannah took her down to the stream, holding tightly to a rope connected to her halter. After a few short sips, she led her back to the barn.

As they reached the open stall, Duckling noticed the carrot in the back of Susie's apron. Reaching for the treat, the horse nudged her human friend's back playfully, making her jump in surprise. Susannah giggled and engaged in a teasing dance with the horse, swooping out of her way a few times, and running back and forth, in and out of the stall. Finally, with a breathless laugh, she slammed her hip into the stall door, closing the horse in, as her arms went around the animal's neck in a hug.

"You silly girl," Susie laughed, tapping the horse's flaxen forehead, feeling the velvety fur, almost the color of melted butter, beneath her finger. "So, you want this carrot, do you?" She pulled out the orange vegetable. "You nearly untied my apron, but I guess you're cooled off enough to eat a little now." With a smile, she fed the carrot to Duckling, keeping her palm flat so she wouldn't get bitten. "I'm glad you like it. You are getting the very, very, very first one. The first thing we grew here, Ducky." Susannah smiled as she pulled her empty hand away. "You deserve it, you good girl." Susannah shifted her body down off the top of the stall door, where she had been leaning, and stepped away. "We'll be back after supper with a nice bucket of water for the night and some hay too, Duckling. Now, you just settle and cool off."

Smiling, Susannah wandered slowly back to the cabin, her mind so full of peaceful joy and plans for supper, that she did not hear the rattle of wood bouncing against wood behind her as she left the barn.

Jeffrey came into the cabin half an hour later with his hair and the tips of his sleeves wet from washing up. Susie had covered the window and was adding the last food item to the table. They enjoyed a long talk about everything Jeff had seen during his day of exploring. Over a plate of slow-roasted jackrabbit, he spoke of spots that would be hard to fence in, places where the woods dipped lower than they had seen before, creating dark hollows and dappled hideaways, the view of the shallow, but sparkly, Platte river and the fish he saw jumping out of it like it was greeting its new visitor. While enjoying, beyond words, her newly harvested carrots, steeped and sprinkled with the lemony taste of dried sumac, Susannah laughed and laughed at Jeff's tales of sighting a prairie dog town, where at least eight of the funny little creatures had stood on their hind legs to warn him off. She dissolved into uncontrollable giggles at Jeff's imitation of the staccato squeaking barks they made at his unwelcome approach. Finally, red-faced from a supper full of amusement and hilarity, Jeff pushed back from the table and stood.

"Well, Susannah, those were easily the best carrots I've ever tasted." He patted his stomach, sighing.

Susie smiled, picking up two pots to wash. "They really do taste better when they come out of our very own garden, don't they?"

"That they do," Jeff said, pulling on his work gloves. "Can't wait to see what comes out of it next."

He ambled out the door to do his final evening chores, as Susannah continued cleaning up the supper dishes.

A moment later, Jeff came back. It was far too soon. Susannah whirled around from the dish basin to see a calm, but concerned look in his eyes.

"What's wrong?" Susannah asked.

"Do you know what happened to Duckling? She's not there."

"I...I...I don't know. What do you mean she's not there?"

Susannah stepped towards him, dripping water from her dishcloth onto the dirt floor.

"When I went in the barn, her stall was wide open and I don't see her anywhere in sight. Did you close the stall door, Susannah?"

"I..yes, of course, I did."

"Did you latch it?"

Silence fell like a blow from a hammer as Susannah gasped. Her heart felt like something had squeezed it. "I....I...don't know." She closed her eyes, thinking back to an hour and a half ago and the light-hearted tussle with the playful horse. She remembered bouncing against the door. She remembered leaning on it and over it, but she couldn't remember latching it. She opened her eyes. "I..I don't think I did, Jeff. Oh, I'm so sorry. It's been a while, she was hot and thirsty. She probably headed to the water and then wandered oh, who knows how far....and it's getting late. Oh, I'm...I'm sorry, Jeff."

Jeffrey sighed. "Well, the only thing to do is go after her." He grabbed his gun, which sent a shiver down Susie's spine as dark possibilities flew unwanted through her mind. "We need that horse," he mumbled, checking that the gun was loaded and putting several bullets in his pocket from a nearby box. "You keep the door string pulled in. It'll be dark soon." Then he turned and left without another word.

Feeling rather stunned, Susannah stumbled to the door and locked herself into the cabin by pulling in the string which allowed people to lift up the door bar from the outside. Then, without really thinking about it, she wandered to the side window, pulled open the covering and soon saw Jeff heading out on the saddled back of Merriment. The dusklight was falling on him and he did not look back. She watched him until he disappeared into the shadowy distance.

That's when what had happened finally sank in. Susannah turned her back to the wall and wrung the dishcloth between her hands until her knuckles turned white. They may have lost Duckling because of her, all because of her. How could she be so careless. Aside from the fact that Duckling was a sweet and dear companion and losing her would be sad, there was even more at stake. A ranch could not function without its horses. Losing one was a heavy blow to a couple starting out. Her mind ran through the long list of things they could no longer do without two horses, like pull the wagon, or drag larger tree trunks, or yank stumps and rocks from the ground. This would slow down the fencing project, hamper future cattle control, limit their ability to travel, and overwork the other mare. Susannah thought of the expense and time of buying and training a new horse. This was a disaster and it was her fault. Anything could happen to Duckling out there in the night and to Jeffrey as he tried to track her. There were snakes finding their way to their burrows right now, head-high tree branches that could not be seen after sunset, holes to step in, rocks to fall on, hills to tumble down. Susannah's whirling thoughts spiraled across every possible pitfall and deadly trap that could be awaiting her husband and their horses in the dark. There were coyotes and wolves out there and even the occasional cougar and bear. She could not stand this. If anything awful happened to Jeff or those beautiful quarter horses because of her, she would never be able to live with herself.

And worst of all, what would Jeff think? He was finally beginning to seem comfortable with her, sometimes even happy. This would set them back. This would prove him right about wives being nothing but problem-makers and burdens. Susannah closed her eyes and prayed desperately that that would not happen. She had always known hardship was a part of the frontier life, any life really, but she had not considered what it would feel like if the little disasters of life were caused by her. There was nothing she could do to fix this. Bursting into tears or collapsing into despair certainly would not help. Susannah slowly finished her praying and swallowed her self-pity. The only thing she could do right now was be useful. So, she cleaned the dishes, the kitchen and the whole house. Trying hard not to give in to more and more worry as the hours dragged on, she put on tea and made a snack for Jeff for when he returned. She laid out more carrots for the horses and set up a bowl of warm water, with soap and cloth nearby, so her husband could wash up again. She left the window open, with its covering pinned to the side. She did every bit of work she could think of, and looked out at the faint moonlight and the blurry dark grassland dozens of times, until finally all she could do was put a lantern in the window to lead Jeff home and settle onto a stool by the fire to sew and wait.

Chapter 11

Half the night ticked by, minute by agonizing minute. Susannah sewed two cloth napkins and started working on a new pair of pants for Jeff. She sewed until her eyes hurt from concentrating in the flickering firelight, and her thumb and forefinger grew numb from endless stitching. When her knuckles began to ache and the needle fell from her grip, she got up and began to pace. After she paced a while, she grabbed the broom and re-swept the already swept floor.

There was something about this waiting, in the night, all alone. Something seemed to break inside her. Susie had always considered herself to be strong. She had endured so much pain and lack of joy in her young life, but this night struck her deep. Her mind wandered down paths she could not find her way back from.

In the beginning, it had been hard to think that Jeffrey could get rid of her anytime he wanted, to have that hanging over her every day, but as time went on she felt that he had let those ideas go. Susie had slowly stopped fearing life in some random town, with a boring thankless job and a back room to sleep in becoming her whole world, a world without him, alone with no one to care about. She had embraced this new life with open arms, let go of her cares and worries, and had been filled with immeasurable happiness. Her cup had overflowed. She should have known that such incredible joy could not last. That wasn't real life. Life was messy and flawed and fraught with ups and downs.

Susannah had learned how to handle injustice and poor

treatment and overwork and loneliness and boredom with life, but she had never experienced the bitterness of making an error that adversely affected her home and her husband. It was a terrible feeling. Her confidence and self esteem plummeted, and left her breathless with the jolt of their shrinking. She had experienced fear since she'd met Jeffrey, both the physical and emotional kind, plus doubt and longing, confusion and worry, but this was something entirely new and darker than all else. She was surprised at how hard it hit her. It was a special kind of misery, bringing thoughts of self-doubt and worthlessness. Suddenly, everything looked different. Her home was a place of endless booby traps. Possible catastrophes were everywhere. Thoughts that she was going to ruin Jeff's dreams, and her own too, bombarded her at every turn. Every task was a potential failure waiting to happen and the night was too silent all of a sudden. Susannah fought hard against the strange melancholy that enveloped her, but her mind kept repeating the same ideas, no matter how many times she pushed them away. She was not right for this life. She was not right for Jeffrey.

Finally, she heard Jeff's voice and a stab of intense relief almost paralyzed her for a second.

"Susannah, I'm back," his voice was wafting through the western window. "Need the light," he explained. "Didn't want to startle you when I took it."

Suddenly, the lantern in the window vanished as Jeffrey pulled it through from the outside. The cabin grew dimmer. Susannah jumped, and then flew to the window in time to see the tiny flame bobbing along towards the barn, looking like it was floating on its own through the darkness. She could just barely make out a sheen of moonlight glinting off the top of Jeff's hair as he walked.

Wanting more than anything to be helpful, Susannah immediately grabbed a stick from the fire and lit their second lantern. She picked up two thick pieces of bread and butter, from the snack she had left prepared on the table, wrapped them in one of the napkins and stuffed them and two carrots into her apron pocket. Then she slung the strap of the canteen she had filled hours ago over her shoulder and headed out, making sure to replace the string through the hole in the door.

Carefully, she made her way over to the barn, finding it because it was the place in the farmyard where the stars were blocked out. It looked like a giant building-shaped splash of black negative space against the night sky. She headed for the weak glow of lantern light escaping the open door.

As Susannah entered, her light added to Jeff's, and everything came into focus. Jeffrey was on his knees in Duckling's stall and the horse was very still. Her head hung low over the stall door and her eyes were drooping with pain and fatigue. Susie hung her lantern on a nail near where Jeff was working.

"Thanks, that's better," he muttered, not taking his eyes off what he was doing.

Seeing that the bridle Jeff had taken with him was now around Duckling's head and the reins of it were tied securely around a post, Susannah felt safe to open the stall door. She knelt down and offered Jeff the canteen.

"Oh, yes!" Jeff said, "I was a fool not to take water. Just rushed out too fast."

He took the canteen, without wiping his hands, and glugged down several long gulps. Susannah could see the horse's blood on Jeff's work gloves. Her eyes smarted with concern and she turned to see what Jeff had been working on. One hand flew to her mouth. Duckling's creamy foreleg was marred by a long scrape or injury of some kind. It was hard to see it well, because it was covered with dried blood and caked with mud and leaves. Jeff had been trying to clean it with a bucket of stream water and a large soft cloth.

She glanced at her husband. His eyes were dull with exhaustion.

His face was pale and his hair was matted with sweat.

"Here, Jeff, you....you need to eat something."

Blinking back tears of shame and worry, Susannah gently untied the bandanna from around Jeff's neck, dipped it in the water bucket and cleaned his hands and face for him. He liked the feeling of her tender caring movements soothing and cooling his skin. Jeff began to relax, shifting his legs into a more comfortable position. Susie draped the napkin across his lap, put one piece of buttered bread on it, and placed the other piece into his left hand. He began to eat while Susannah took hold of the large rag he'd been using and carefully cleaned off Duckling's leg, little by little.

After a few bites, Jeff began to tell her about his search.

"I was surprised how much heat the ground held onto for the first few hours after sunset. I'll be happy when autumn comes." He took another bite. "The moon was just a sliver and I couldn't make out much at all after the last of the light faded from the sky. I really should have taken a lantern, but every time I thought that I'd better head home and look for Ducky after daybreak, I'd hear something and think 'maybe that's her'." He took another drink of water. "If she wasn't so brightly colored, I'd have never seen her, but that little bit of moonlight bounced right off that blonde hair of hers... and it's a good thing she's so loyal too. She just came right to me, when some horses would have been jittery and spooked after being lost like that and it being so dark and all...," he paused, looking at the gash that was appearing beneath the dirt on Duckling's leg. "I...well, I couldn't see nothin' out there, but I could tell she was limping, so we came home real slow-like, but I didn't see what the problem was 'til we got here."

"Well, she doesn't seem snake-bit. Her eyes aren't glassy and she isn't shivering with poison." Susannah wiped off a little more mud. "Yeah, now that I've got it just about cleaned out, it looks like just a bad scrape. It isn't broken," Susannah mumbled, trying to keep the tremble out of her voice. "And...and it's not very swollen. I....I think it's just a cut from a stumble or from scraping a sharp rock or log. I don't see any coyote teeth marks or nothin'," She turned her eyes on Jeff and finally couldn't keep them from filling with tears. "Oh, Jeff, you don't think she'll be lame, do you? I'm so sorry. It's all my fault."

"Well, that it is, but there isn't any point in upsetting yourself over it. That won't help." The moment the words came out, he knew they were the wrong ones. Never in his life had Jeff had to comfort someone else and he had absolutely no such skills. It was going to take trial and error and practice. He felt like a blind man fumbling for the wall. He searched his mind for better words, but not much came to mind. He hated seeing Susannah's tears and the sound of anguish in her voice was painful, but he had no idea how to make her feel better. "Look, whether she's lame or not is something only time will tell." Jeff stood up, leaving Susie sprawled in the dusty barn floor with sprigs of straw all over her skirt. He had to get out of there and think. He had never felt what she was making him feel, with those shining mournful eyes brimming with tears and remorse. It was awful. "I'm going to go get....um....get some bandages, yeah and....and you just stay here and keep her calm." The napkin fell from his legs, forgotten, as he all but ran from the barn, barely remembering to grab a lantern as he went.

Jeffrey headed over to the cabin and rummaged around through the neatly folded fabrics that Susie kept under the bed for sewing. He found a large piece of soft white cloth leftover from when she had made sheets and pillowcases for their bed. After finding it, he sat on the floor for a long moment, holding the material in his lap. Thoughts were flying through his mind so fast that he could not catch them. They could have lost the horse, they still might. That would be a huge blow to the ranch and yet, that did not seem to hit him as hard as seeing Susie's tears. That sight had punched him right in the gut. He did not care that she had left the stall door open. He could have done the same, anyone could. Things like this happened in life. He certainly wasn't mad about it, but he didn't know how to tell her that it was ok. Every time Jeff opened his mouth, the wrong thing came out. Frustrated, Jeff squeezed the fabric between his fists. What kind of a husband couldn't even comfort his wife? Wasn't that a huge part of the job description? He suddenly felt very small and inadequate. He was used to failure. It was how one learned, but breaking things, losing things, saying the wrong words, or stupidly keeping all your money in one place and nearly losing everything, were the kind of failures he had grown used to in life. They had helped him grow, but this felt very different. He had developed a deep caring for Susannah that had crept over him slowly, and not being able to make her happy in this rough life he had brought her to, was surprisingly painful. He had never expected to feel such things.

Jeff shook his head and stood up. These thoughts were not getting him anywhere. No solutions were appearing. He picked up Susie's sewing basket and took it to the table. He fished out a couple of safety pins and laid them on top of the fabric, then he pulled his knife out of the sheath at his hip, grabbed the lantern and headed outside. A moment later, he was back with an armload of purple coneflowers that had been growing along the back of the cabin. Hesitating to face his wife again, he took a deep breath, picked up the fabric and pins and forced himself to head back to the barn.

Since he had not come up with anything comforting to say, Jeff decided to focus on the horse. He marched into the barn, and dove into giving directions. Susie was standing rubbing Duckling's nose. Both horses had the remnants of carrots in their mouths. Susannah turned to look at Jeff, but didn't say anything.

"I'm going to start tearing this into bandages," he began. "I left a pile of coneflowers on the table. I need you to mash them down, everything but the stems, and bring the paste out to me when it's spreadable."

Susannah looked a little startled. "Um....ok, Jeff." She started to leave.

"And...uh...the other day," his voice stopped her in her tracks, "Didn't I see you making some oil from those evening primroses that grow on the other side of the creek?"

"Uh...the yellow ones, yes. When I was a little girl, my mother taught me to use primrose oil on..um...skin rashes and things like that."

"Yeah, you can put some in the paste to make it smoother, if you need to." He started to spread out the white fabric in his hands. "I saw my grandmother do it like that."

"Um...ok, sure, Jeff."

Susannah left and Jeffrey felt relieved that she was gone.

***

Susannah was glad to have something to do. Being useful and busy were all that was going to keep her from falling apart. She, of course, had wiped away her tears almost immediately, in the barn earlier, but it had been too late. Jeff had seen them. He already thought wives were a hassle, now she had shown him that she was weak and sappy. She must be strong. That was all she could think of right now. Just be strong and quiet. Be helpful and hardworking and make things better in any possible way.

Setting her lantern on the table, she lit several candles around the room and set to work. She had no idea why Jeff needed coneflower mush, but she assumed it would somehow be good for Ducky's wound. So, she would make him the best paste she could possibly make. Quickly, she stripped the stems of their leaves, flowers and roots and tossed the stems in the waste bucket. Then, she made short work of chopping the plant pieces into tiny bits. With her hands, Susie tossed together the pastel pinkish-violet bits of petals with the moist grass-colored leaf debris and the miniscule pieces of pale root, until it was all well mixed. Then, with a few drops of evening primrose oil, she smashed handfuls of the multi-hued roughage between her mortar and pestle with vigor, scooping each batch into a bowl until her arms were weary and the whole pile had been turned into a creamy dark green paste. It looked like some kind of slime from a swamp, but she had a feeling it was full of nutrients and things beyond her comprehension.

Carrying the bowl, and one of her small spoons, she rushed over to the barn and found Jeff there, patting Ducky's neck, and feeding her handfuls of hay. A dozen strips of bandage hung over the stall door.

"Ah, here we go, Ducky," Jeff said taking the bowl and spoon. "This will make you feel better." He began to apply the sticky goop to Duckling's injury. The tired horse stood very still. Susannah knelt down with a bandage in her hand. "It's an old Indian remedy my Grandma taught me," Jeff mumbled absentmindedly, as his eyes concentrated hard on what he was doing.

Soon, the poultice was applied and Susannah had wrapped the whole length of the wound with the nice clean bandage, sealing the soothing flower-paste inside and securing the cloth, carefully, with the safety pins. Then they hung buckets of water for both cooled-down horses to drink from and carried the lanterns back to the cabin.

Jeff pulled in the string to secure the house for what was left of the night and headed to the waiting wash bowl to clean the residue of the coneflower poultice off of his hands. Susannah walked to the hearth and retrieved a small pot she had left near the edge to stay warm.

"Here," she said softly. "Have some tea."

She poured him a tin cup full of the hot drink she had prepared hours ago and stirred in one spoonful of sugar, just as he liked it. Then she went over to the low shelf by the window where she washed dishes. Her mortar, pestle and knife had been left soaking in the basin there. She began to scrub them.

Jeff stared at her, but couldn't find any words. He was too worried about saying the wrong thing again. He dried his hands on the towel Susie had left by the soap and picked up his tea. After a sip, he took his wife's tin cup off of its hook, poured tea for her and stirred in the two spoonfuls of sugar that he knew she liked. He walked over and handed it to her. She met his eyes and hers were dark and unhappy. Pulling her hands out of the wash water, she mumbled a thank you, sipped his offering twice and then set the cup aside and returned to her work.

Jeff knew that now that they were coming down off the recent crisis and alone in the quietness left behind, he could not stay silent. Wouldn't that make Susie feel worse? He had to say something, but he didn't know what.

"It was an accident, Susie."

Susannah sighed. She did not turn to look at him. "I hurt that horse. You said yourself, it was my fault,… and it could cost us so much. I don't know how I'll ever make that up to you."

"First of all," Jeff was talking to Susannah's back, "You don't have to make anything up to anyone, and you did not hurt that horse. It just happened and it was an accident. It could have just as easily happened to me. I have left stall doors open before, you know. Every kid has—"

"I'm not a kid," Susannah interrupted softly. He could barely make out her response. "It was a stupid mistake for a grown woman. I need to be more careful. I have to be." She was muttering to herself. Jeff didn't even hear the last part.

"Secondly," Jeff continued, because he didn't know what else to do, "We don't know if it will cost us anything until we see how Duckling heals. She could be perfectly fine. So, lets not borrow trouble."

Jeff suddenly clamped his mouth shut. Once again, he was saying unhelpful things. He had not learned enough kindness in his life. It was a terrible thing to be lacking. As Susannah

ARRANGED

continued to scrub and scrub, Jeff closed his eyes and wracked his brain, trying to think of anytime he had been in a similar situation. Had anyone ever comforted him? Certainly not his selfish mother or his testy arrogant father. Thinking back further and further into the past, Jeff finally pulled up a fragment of a memory that might help.

"You know, once, when I was eight, I started a stampede on my Grandpa's ranch. It was my first trip there. I had no idea what I was doing. Didn't know how to behave around cattle." Jeff sighed, remembering. "Several cows were lost. You want to talk about cost? Whooo-eee, I cost my grandparents a lot of money that day. This was back before Grandma died. I still remember the way she shook her head at me and called me a 'passel of trouble'. Then she just headed inside to make supper for all the poor ranch hands that had to clean up my mess." Jeff took a step closer to Susannah. She finally set the over scrubbed items on a towel to dry, but she did not turn to look at him. "You know what Grandpa said? He just ambled over to me and leaned on the fence, like he always did, and said, 'You make mistakes and, if you live, you learn." Jeff paused for a moment, remembering his patient, hard-working grandfather. That had been the first time anyone had ever reacted to his errors in a calm, useful, and not furious, way. His grandpa's words were all he could think of to give Susannah. "I....I, well, I've always remembered what he said, Susie."

"You do a good job living by what he said, Jeff." Susannah's voice was soft and kind. It floated out the window in front of her, into the night air. "You learn and grow very well. It's one of the things I admire about you."

Susannah sounded sad and confused and it was making Jeff feel the same way. He had no idea how to respond to what she had just said. Nothing he was doing was working. He wanted to cheer her up, to make her stop blaming herself, to help her smile again. Perhaps a change of subject would help. That was something he had tried often, when his parents were arguing. He would bring up a new subject and try to redirect everyone's thoughts. Perhaps that old habit would work now with Susannah. His mind floundered around, until his gaze fell on the stone pestle, drying at his wife's side. He thought of the poultice they had made.

"You know, my grandmother was a highly educated woman, and she didn't grow up in Texas. She went to The Linden Wood School for Girls over in Missouri. She used to tell me it was the very first establishment of higher education for women west of the Mississippi River. She was proud of that." He turned to look at Susannah's back. Wisps of her rosy-dark hair were curling around her collar. "I wish I had remembered her more when I first met you -- remembered what some woman can be like, instead of always comparing every girl to my mother and her rude friends." He took a step closer to Susie and leaned on the wall nearby, feeling the hot tea warming his hands through the cup he held. "Grandma studied botany."

"What's that?" Susannah whispered, looking down at the basin of dirty water in front of her.

"It's the study of plants," Jeff answered. "She was a lot like you. You like plants too."

"I try to like all living things....," Susie's voice drifted away, as she looked back up at the window again. Her sad eyes gazed from the barn to the moon and then out across the open prairie grasses rustling in the quiet night wind.

"Yeah, you two would have gotten along real well," Jeff continued. "She was always tellin' me their Latin names,...the names of the plants, I mean. I only remember bits and pieces. I was always more interested in the cattle, but I remember this one," he said, picking up a lost coneflower that had fallen in the corner and missed being turned into goo. He twirled it in between his fingers and didn't even realize he was approaching close to Susie as he spoke. "Echinacea, she called it."

He gently tucked the pretty blossom behind Susannah's ear,

letting his fingers run down the side of her face. Her body relaxed a little, finally. He didn't plan to do that. It had just sort of happened without his consciously choosing it, but he liked, so much, the way her soft skin felt beneath his touch, and he was very glad to finally see her letting go of a little of the tension she had been holding.

"Echinacea…," Susannah repeated quietly, fingering the petals in her hair. She was finally looking at him and he started to breathe easier. He never again wanted to spend so long, with her in the same room, without her eyes looking into his.

"Yeah," he nodded, "I remember it because it's good for wounds for people and horses. They had those same flowers in Texas. They're everywhere. They're good for pain and they prevent infection. So, I'm betting on Grandma. I'm betting that Ducky is going to be just fine, Susie."

Susannah sighed and turned her eyes away again. "That's nice, Jeff, I like to learn stuff like that…thank you for telling me…I have a lot to learn. I know that."

Again, she would not look at him. He hated it. For one moment, he had thought he was actually consoling her, but now, she seemed closed off again.

"You're exhausted," he mumbled, feeling as sorrowful as his wife. "I am too. Let's just get some sleep. We can check on Ducky after daybreak and everything will feel better in the sunshine."

He covered the window and walked around blowing out candles and lanterns one by one. Susannah did not budge from her spot by the window. Jeff didn't bother to change clothes, since they wouldn't be resting for long. He just slipped off his shoes and crawled into bed. The cabin was dark now, lit only by the faint flickers of the low fire in the fireplace. As he watched, Susannah's shadowy form slowly removed her shoes, like he had, walked rather haltingly over to the bed, and finally climbed in next to him. For the first time, he did not turn to the wall. Instead, he lay staring at the back of her head, surprised at how much he wanted to pull the pins from her russet hair and bury his fingers in it, but he could sense that she was crying softly and trying not to let him hear, so he remained still and drifted to sleep thinking of her.

Chapter 12

A few more weeks went by and the summer passed its peak. The temperatures that had been hanging on tight, making everything sweat, began to wane just a little. Susannah worked harder than ever at everything she did, but the joy seemed to have gone out of her. She no longer took pride in her little accomplishments or relished the quiet moments of planning and organizing that she used to love. Jeff watched her from afar, in the mornings and evenings, wishing that she would talk a little more. She had always been a fairly quiet person, but not so totally silent, only responding when spoken to and then only with a few words. She no longer told him things about her day or laughed at his stories about his day. He talked and talked the evenings away, trying to get some kind of rise out of her, but nothing worked. She seemed lost in strange thoughts. He could see them whirling behind her eyes and wondered what they were.

The day after Duckling's accident, he had come into the cabin in the middle of the afternoon to bring Susannah a gift. After hours of thought, it had occurred to him that perhaps giving her a present would cheer her up. He told her that he had noticed that she always used the same tiny spoons that they ate their soup with, to cook and mix batter and stir pots on the fire. He had carved her a very nice wooden spoon with a long handle. It was a copy of the one Cooky had used on the cattle drives Jeff had ridden on down in Texas. When he had offered it to her, she had approached him and put her hands over his. She looked into his eyes and thanked him. She said it was a wonderful spoon and perfect for cooking. She told him he was very kind, but she did not smile, and her eyes seemed to say, 'I don't deserve this'.

It was hard for Jeff to believe, at first, but he missed the way she used to be. He never would have thought that he could grow to like the conversation and smiles or a wife he never wanted, but it had happened. She had somehow tiptoed into his heart, one tiny step at a time, like a kitten approaching its prey. Who knew that a relationship could develop with such stealth that he didn't even realize it was happening. When he tried to think about it too much, he got all confused and pushed the thoughts away. He didn't know exactly what he felt, but he wasn't ready to except whatever it was. All he knew for certain, was that he wanted Susie to smile again.

Susannah spent her days thinking. Duckling's leg was getting better and she was immensely grateful for that, but just because a full recovery for the horse might be possible, that did not erase the fact that Susannah had nearly cost Jeff his livelihood. This ranch could have failed before it had even begun because of her expensive mistake. She had never had so much depending on her before. Such responsibility had not entered into the naïve plans she had made growing up. How could she have been so childish? So filled with rosy dreams of pillowy bright possibilities, that she never even considered the dark parts of life, the struggles, the worries and failures? She felt stupid and small.

Susannah tried to tell herself that she was overreacting. So she had left a stall door open, and it had caused a chain reaction of potential disaster. It was a mistake. Mistakes were part of life, right? It wasn't like she had never made one before. Why was this so different? As she took a smoking stick outside to gather honey, or wove a new basket for foraging berries and herbs, her mind would not stop whirring. As she tended the garden, kneaded bread or scrubbed laundry each day, the same thoughts repeated over and over in her head.

Why was this hitting her so hard? Susannah knew exactly why.

She had practically forced herself upon this ranch. She had gone against Jeff's wishes by coming here instead of letting him leave her behind. Now, Jeff was dealing with whatever harm she did to his life without having chosen to do so. He had not wanted her. He still didn't. If they were a normal couple, she could have accepted her errors with peace, learned from them and moved on, because her husband would have been someone who chose her and knew that would come with consequences. They would have been in a life that they had decided on together, knowing there would be struggles and mistakes, and being ok with that. 'Come what may', they would have said, together, and jumped into a new world with eyes wide open. But that is not what had happened.

Susannah felt like she had been in denial for months. She had told herself, from the beginning, that she was going to be good for Jeff, good for his ranch. She had been so sure that she would enhance his life, make his home better, and eventually he would see that her choice to stay with him, against his will, had been a good thing. Now, Susie realized how selfish that had been. She had wanted this life so much that she had put herself above another person. Before he had been forced to marry her, Jeffrey Bridges had had so many dreams and plans, all securely in place, drafted out so carefully in his mind. She had ruined all of that and she could not take it back.

It wasn't the incident with Duckling that was weighing on Susie. It was what the event represented. Her mistake, and its aftermath, had made her see things she had been blind to. In those early days, Susannah had ignored the wrongness of what she was doing because for the first time in her life, she had thought only about herself. As time went on, she had grown to care so much about her husband, and now her own selfish desires were slipping away, overshadowed by something she'd been defining in her heart for a while now.

Susannah's hands stopped pounding the bread dough into the table in front of her. She stared at the long wooden spoon that

Jeff had made her, that sat crusty with flour in her mixing bowl. She couldn't hide it from herself anymore. She loved Jeffrey. She did. She was sure of it. That was why she was so unhappy. It was because she realized that she had forced her way into his life, and he had never wanted her, and that mattered now, because she loved him. She did not want to keep burdening him, saddling him with a marriage he never asked for. When she loved someone, she had to help them, and put them first, and do what was right for them and she so deeply wanted to do that, but she did not know how.

There was nothing she could do now. She was here. She and Jeffrey were stuck with each other. Somehow, she had to move on past the mistakes she had made and the dark feelings that filled her days. She had to keep moving forward day by day, trying not to get in Jeff's way. What else could she do?

***

One day, in early September, Jeff came home to find Susannah sewing at the table, with the supper all laid out. She did not usually sew at mealtime and her face was blotchy and red from crying, although her eyes were dry now. The window covering was open, when it was usually closed by now, and he could sense a faint burnt stench in the air. Alarmed, he glanced around. There were pieces of blackened cloth in the waste bucket, a slash of singed wall where the shelf to the right of the fireplace had been and Susannah was stitching a brand new sleeve onto her second dress.

"Susie!" he exclaimed, jumping to her side. "What happened?!"

Susannah kept sewing and did not meet his eyes. Her answer came out in short clipped phrases as her needle kept going in and out of the cloth in her lap.

"I was reaching for the stew." Through her fingers the thread slid and pulled, back and forth. "My sleeve caught fire." The needle clacked against her thimble as she started another stitch. "I jumped up." Jeff listened patiently as he watched her shift the cloth and tie a knot. "It engulfed my arm, and as I ran I bounced off the wall." She set down her needle and broke off the extra thread with her teeth. Jeffrey grabbed her arm and shoved up the sleeve. She just kept talking, staring ahead at the charred spot on the wall. "I turned and raced to the dishwater and doused my arm." Jeff could see slightly reddened splotches on the skin of Susannah's arm, but the injury was minor. She pulled her arm free and started re-threading her needle. "I...I...um," she cleared her throat and continued, "I turned back around and the wall was on fire." She drove her needle back into the fabric. "It was the spot I had bounced into." Jeff finally reached down and removed the dress from her lap. She did not protest as he slipped the needle from her fingers and dropped it into her sewing basket. Her eyes returned to the scorch mark on the log wall. "It destroyed the little shelf there. I threw the dishwater at it."

"And you put it out," Jeff finished. "Susie, we need to put something on your arm." He started glancing around at all the little bowls and bags of things that Susannah kept on shelves, the re-used jars of this and that, the herbs drying as they hung from the ceiling.

"I'm fine," she mumbled. "It's no worse than a sunburn, didn't break the skin—"

"Yeah, it just singed it, Susie!" Jeff interrupted, upset. "Susannah your arm got burned, with...with fire, Susie! And...and I'm going to put something on it!"

He began to pace back and forth from one shelve to another. Susannah just sat, unmoving in her chair, staring at the burn mark in the front corner. Finally, he grabbed an old fruit jar that now held evening primrose oil. Then he changed his mind, slammed the jar back down and grabbed a bowl containing fresh honeycomb. Susannah's arm was long cooled, and now it just needed something to soothe the skin and keep it moisturized and sealed from debris. He was overdoing it, as the wound was negligible, but he had to do something. He returned to

Susannah, rolled up her sleeve and tucked it in at the shoulder. Then he began dipping his fingers into the honeycomb cells, digging out the gooey honey and spreading it gently over the reddened skin.

Susannah was staring down at her lap now. "I could have burned your house down, Jeffrey." Her voice came out in a deathly quiet whisper.

"Women have been catching their dresses in fireplaces since time immemorial, Susannah. It happens." He continued applying the sticky honey to the tender spots on his wife's arm. "You know, I've actually been thinking of putting in a window right there, so we can see both east and west. So, there's no harm done really. I'll just cut that spot right out and the whole wall will be like new."

Susannah's head lowered even further, until her chin touched her chest. She was not listening. "I could have burned your house down," she repeated.

Jeffrey sighed and tilted her face up with his clean hand until he forced her eyes to meet his. "It's *our* house, Susie. *Our* house, and if you had burned it down, do you know what I would have done?" She shook her head. "Well, I would have just built us another one, that's all. I'm just so glad that you're all right."

Jeff was surprised at how much he meant that. He never knew how quickly he could get attached to someone, but he was attached to this girl, his wife. She was changing him. He wasn't angry about the fire or the injured horse. He didn't even care about the whole ranch as much as he cared about Susannah. That revelation inside his mind startled and scared him. What was happening to him? He spend the rest of the evening in silence, thinking about it, as they ate a quiet meal and went silently to bed.

***

The day after the fire, Jeffrey knocked and scraped the mud

mortar out of a spot on the wall beside the fire damage, using his homemade wooden mallet and his largest chisel. He hacked a little at the area with his hatchet until he made a hole big enough to insert his saw. Then he sawed away at the scorched area, creating a nice straight-edged window. Pretty soon, it looked like there had never been a fire at all.

"It's a lovely window, Jeffrey," Susannah said softly, when he showed it to her, but inside her head she was thinking how she wished her husband had not had to swoop in and fix her mistakes. She stared at the open-air window and wondered if every time she looked at it, it would remind her of her failures.

It was very clear to Jeffrey that his wife had spiraled into some kind of depression, but he didn't know how to fix her and life had to go on. If he concentrated on work, time would pass, and time was supposed to heal everything, right? So, he started to plan the next step in developing his ranch.

That night, he watched as Susannah covered the westward window with its screen of thin greased paper. Then, she moved to the new window, on the eastern wall, and pinned up a fresh sheet of the same paper, that she had just prepared with deer fat.

"Susie, listen," he started, "I think we're ready for a supply run. I want to buy glass for our windows, and we need more food for winter and now that we have a barn, I think it's time we got ourselves a milk cow."

Susannah sighed as she began to bring supper items to the table. Jeffrey's nostrils filled with the rich scents of venison steaks and roasted potatoes freshly harvested from the garden.

"But, didn't you say that Duckling's leg isn't quite ready for traveling yet?" Susannah asked, sitting down and putting fresh biscuits on each plate. "She can't haul a wagon, can she?"

Jeffrey paused the conversation to pray for the food, then began cutting his meat. "No, she's going to be just fine, but, you're right, she can't haul a wagon just yet, but it could start getting cold soon. I'm not familiar enough with the seasons around here yet, and I don't want to take any chances." He took a bite of a dry biscuit. "Just think, you could finally make your own butter, anytime you want. I know you've run out of the batch that Ashley brought you at the barn raising." He took a bite of potatoes, marveling at Susie's ability to season food so scrumptiously. He didn't even know the names of the herbs and spices that encrusted these potatoes, but he loved their tantalizing flavors. "And you'd have milk for baking cakes and things, and you'd have cream. Just think, when the snows come, we could mix up some ice cream." His eyes rolled with pleasure as he took another bite of the meal. "Mmmm, Susie, this supper is delicious as usual. Don't know how I ever lived without your cooking."

Susannah did not acknowledge the compliment. She sat barely touching her food. "So, you'll just take Merri, then? Into North Platte?" Jeff nodded yes, with his mouth full of potatoes. "And me?"

Jeff swallowed his bite of food. "You'll…uh…stay here."

Susie nodded slowly, pushing her venison back and forth with her fork. "I can stay here," she repeated quietly.

"I mean, unless you really don't want to," Jeffrey said, staring at her with concern in his eyes. "I suppose I could take you over to stay with the Andersons, if you like. They won't mind, and we could ride double that far." He skewered a piece of meat and raised it towards his lips. "We haven't had any trouble around here. It's a real quiet area. I've thought about it. The Sioux have kept to the treaty and stayed on the other side of the river, no aggressive neighbors have showed themselves and even the animals have been peaceful so far. I'm sure the ranch would be fine if we left it empty for a fortnight. In fact, without the wagon, it won't even take that long. I'd just have to think of what to do with Duckling."

"Oh, no, no." Susannah didn't want to be a bother of any kind.

"I'm about to harvest the three sisters--,"

"The what now?" Jeff asked, curious. Being interested in only cattle since boyhood, and being the son of a banker, he knew far too little about growing food. He had a sudden thought about how he could have ever believed he could make it out here without a wife.

"The corn, squash and beans," Susannah answered, looking at him. A little of her old spark came into her voice as she talked about the garden she loved. "They sort of grow together and help each other. Anyway, the corn needs a little longer, but the squash and beans can't wait anymore. Especially, if we get a frost. They'd be ruined." Her voice lowered again and she looked down at her barely touched food. "And…you know…someone has to stay and look after Ducky, so, I'll be just fine, I'm sure."

"You know," Jeffrey had a sudden idea, "I really should think about digging you a root cellar to store your vegetables in. It will keep them cool, so they'll last longer." He waited, hoping the thought would make her smile.

Susannah did not smile (he was starting to wonder if she had forgotten how), but she did reach out and put her hand over his for an all too brief moment. "I think that would be lovely," she said in her so-soft voice. "Thank you for thinking of it."

He smiled, staring into her eyes, but his grin faded when she pulled her hand away and looked back down at her hardly touched food.

"Will you be bringing the cattle back?" she asked, after a silent moment had passed.

"Well, no, not this time." Jeffrey picked up his biscuit and stared at its crusty golden top. "I still haven't gotten a bunkhouse built for the hands and I'm afraid I was a little too ambitious with my fence-building plans." He looked over at her. "I'm..uh…not even close to being done. I really should have hired some help." He took a bite of the biscuit and set it back down as he chewed.

When he had swallowed, he continued. "The cattle will just have to wait until spring. It's not the end of the world."

"I've slowed you down," Susannah mumbled, stabbing a potato, then dropping it back onto the plate.

"What? Are you kidding me?" Jeff was genuinely surprised at the notion. "I'd be so much further behind without you. Why, I would have had to put in that garden myself, or I'd have half starved by now, and the cabin would have taken twice as long. It never even occurred to me that a woman could be so much help in building a cabin." He tried to lighten the mood with a chuckle, but it fell flat, when Susie didn't even look up. "Hey, remember how much help you were with the corral?" he went on. "We got that thing up in a day. It would have taken me three, by myself. Why, without you here, I would have barely gotten started on the fencing. I'd still be working on it next summer." Jeffrey paused. He was having a revelation. How could he have ever thought that building a ranch would have been easier by himself? He could see now how truly foolish that idea had been. He reached over and captured Susannah's hand in his own. "I know I was hoping to get the cattle this fall, but that was just inexperience talking. I can see that now, and, Susie, without you here, I wouldn't even be ready for cattle in the spring." He rubbed his hand back and forth across the soft skin on the back of her hand. "You've been a big help. Truly, you have. I had no idea how much help a wife could be, really, Susie."

"You don't have to say that," Susie whispered.

"It's the truth," Jeff released her and returned to his food.

No, it's not the truth, Susie thought, as she watched her husband eat. She stared at his bent head, leaning over his food, and felt that his words were just an attempt to reassure another human being and bury his own real desire to be alone and have his old dreams back. He was just becoming comfortable enough with her to start letting his true kindness show. That was all this was, and that very kindness actually hurt worse than if he had not tried to comfort her. It made her love him more, and that just increased all the different aches and confusions roiling around inside her.

Chapter 13

Two days later, Jeffrey had everything, but himself, ready to leave for his journey to North Platte. He and his wife stood outside the cabin, with Merriment at their side.

Susannah stared at her shoes, sweeping her foot back and forth across a loose pebble, moving it a little each time. "Are you sure you want to leave me here alone?" she mumbled under her breath. "I might destroy the place." Her foot stopped suddenly. She had not meant to speak out loud. Her bitter thoughts had tumbled out of her mouth unbidden. She peeked upward to see if Jeffrey had heard. He had.

Jeff finished tucking Susannah's letters to her cousins into his saddle bag and turned toward his wife. "Don't say that," he said with a disappointed sigh. "You fit beautifully here, Susannah. You're just going through a rough patch. Maybe some new supplies and a nice little cow will lift your spirits, or maybe you'll cheer up later in the year, when you see this place covered in sparkly snow, but whatever it takes, in time, you will feel better. You love it here."

I do, she thought, but he doesn't love me being here. He doesn't love me or my presence and he never will. He's just learned how to bury that fact, and not show it anymore, like he did in the early days. Susannah felt that at least those days had been honest. At least she had felt like she was on solid ground back then, and knew her own heart and could see her path ahead. Lately, she could see nothing, but uncertainty and gloom. It had been less than six months, but it seemed like an eternity ago, that she had felt peacefully resigned to marry a practical stranger and run away to an unknown life with him, without caring much about his feelings. Things were so different now.

"I'll stop by the Andersons' on my way," Jeffrey's voice broke into Susie's dark reverie, as he pulled on his gloves. "So, they'll know you're alone. If, for some reason, I don't come back by their place in timely fashion, they'll know to come check on you. Of course, Duckling will be ready for riding in maybe four or five more days. So, you could always ride out on her if you needed help."

"I'll be just fine," Susie said, looking up at him. "Don't worry about me. Since we started, you've worried enough about a woman you didn't want to bring with you. Just take this as a chance to feel alone for a while, you know, like you planned."

Jeffrey stopped moving and stared at her. He had no idea how to respond to what she had just said. There, technically, wasn't anything wrong in her words, but it felt wrong to him anyway. Finally, she let him off the hook for an answer, by changing the subject.

"I still think you should take the rifle with you."

"No, we've been over this." He turned to check the cinch and girth under Merriment's belly one last time. "It's just like when I'm out on the range. I'll be on my horse or near it, which means I'll be up high, out of the range of an animal's jaws, and also able to ride away from one. You'll be out and about, right on the ground within a predator's grasp, and just because we haven't seen a wolf or a coyote yet, doesn't mean one can't wander by any day. I hear them all the time at night, and there's always the rattlers." He finished what he was doing and turned back to her. "So, you keep the rifle, just like you do when I'm out fencing. Besides, what kind of a husband takes the gun for himself and leaves his wife defenseless?" He shook his head. "Yeah, that's just not going to happen."

"Well, all right then." Susannah's arms dropped to her sides in acceptance. "I'll keep it loaded and in arm's reach at all times, just like you taught me."

Jeffrey nodded his satisfaction. "And I think I'll look around for another gun in town. Maybe I can get a cheap one used, and then we'll have two." He stepped closer to her and lowered his voice. "Now, you just start thinking of a name for our little cow and you stay safe and close to the house."

"I won't go any further than the barn and the stream," she said, putting her hands over his in reassurance.

"You promise?" he said, gently squeezing her fingers and gazing into her face. "No exploring? No foraging in the woods?"

"I promise," she declared, returning his gaze.

A moment of quiet passed, slow and languid. Breezes blew the prairie grasses all around them and a wood thrush greeted them with its high-pitched song, as it landed on the edge of the cabin's bark roof. The sun was rising over Jeff's right shoulder, filling the sky with lavenders and mellow burning oranges. The young man stood stiller than he ever had, focused on his wife's soft skin between his palms. He didn't know how to leave her, he only knew that he didn't want to. A dozen ways to stay, or take her with him, ran through Jeff's mind, but eventually, he forced himself to take a deep breath and release her fingers from his. He stepped back. His hands felt cold from the absence of hers. He kept looking at her pretty glowing eyes and her loose early-morning hair, blowing in auburn streaks into the wind, like someone had dipped a paintbrush into smoldering coals and brushstroked their warm color across the sky beside her head. He stumbled backwards into his horse and then abruptly mounted up to cover his discomfort.

"Um, I'll…uh….I'll be back, Susie-girl. I'll be back as soon as I can." He didn't know what else to say, so he nudged the horse with his heels and rode off, thinking of a thousand better goodbyes as he went, but the worst regret of them all was a sudden wish that tugged at him out of the blue. As he crested the big hill and glanced back, realizing painfully that he couldn't see his wife anymore, he wished with all his heart that he had hugged her goodbye.

***

The dozen days that Jeffrey was away from home were strange for both him and Susannah.

In the lovely daytime of almost autumn, as the grass yellowed out, the mornings turned crisp and a few trees changed their hues, Susie actually managed to let go of some of her dark feelings, just a little. Peace began to return. Being away from Jeff was filled with an odd mix of longing for him and being glad he was not there to disappoint. She felt like she was living in a temporary reprieve from all her problems. She basked in long quiet afternoons, good work to do and the beautiful countryside around her, as the prairie dogs grew pudgier preparing for the coming cold, and the dying flowers blew their petals into the cool breezes. Jeff was right, she loved this place and, during the days, it felt wonderful to just set aside her doubts and guilt and simply be free in her dream life. She took care of Duckling, bathed in the stream, laundered all their clothes and blankets, harvested the squash and beans, started the winter canning and did dozens of other tasks that were filled with the joy they used to carry. She managed to kill a copperhead with her hoe and even endured a late summer storm, that rattled the branch-made fencing around her garden and whipped howling gales around her little cabin. These things did not bother her. Instead, they reminded her of the endurance that she had always believed to be her strength. Coming out of little hardships feeling brave and sturdy, helped to return some of Susannah's lost confidence. She treasured her days, even with the intense ache of missing her favorite person in the world. He would return, she told herself. It wouldn't be long.

The nights, however, were a different story altogether. Susie lay alone in the unnerving stillness, watching the glow of moonlight through the greased paper over the westward window, and listening to the crackle of the dying hearthfire and the distant baying of wolves. She was not frightened of the deep dark of open country or the unidentified rustles that wafted over from the woods. She loved the nighttime as much as the day, out here in this dreamed-of wild land she had always wanted to live in, but what she did not love were the thoughts that returned to her heart in the quiet, and in the loneliness of Jeff's absence that grew so much worse after nightfall.

In the hush of those long twilights, she thought endlessly of her husband. She counted the infinite things she loved about him: his slowly unfolding kindness, his gentle touches, his homey life-building skills that had given her her dreams, his voice, his face, his presence at her side. She had grown to love just about everything about Jeffrey and the full realization of all that that meant was gradually unfurling inside her, but most of all, in the interminable lonesomeness of night, Susie's mind ran over and over all the ways that she had shattered Jeff's dreams and changed his plans, all the ways she had been selfish and wrong. Each morning she awoke still tired, and determined to find a way to fix what she had done, but she still knew no solution to her error. She could not unmarry Jeff. She could not go back in time. There was nothing to do, but be the best and most quiet-as-a-mouse, out-of-the-way wife that she could possibly be, just as she had promised in the beginning, but with her recent failures, she worried that she could never reach that goal.

In all her years of dreaming, she had always told herself that the husband part of her dreams was incidental and that she did not really care what kind of husband she had. As long as he didn't hurt her, she would throw herself into building her own little world in her long imagined kitchen and garden, revel in the absence of her unkind, unfeeling aunt and uncle, and be content with something of her own for the first time in her life. For years, she had believed that this dream was realistic, that binding herself to some man was just a way out of her dreary life, but as she lay all alone now, feeling Jeff's absence keenly, running over their conversations in her mind, recalling his demeanor, the looks in his eyes, she knew that her husband wasn't just a filler in her plans. She had known it for a long time now, and she looked back on that puerile girl, who had believed such a thing, and called her a fool.

Jeffrey was a real person, a huge part of this world Susannah had wanted to build. He was changing, in ways he shouldn't have to, to fit her into this life she never deserved, and she needed to change too. How could she have ever thought that she would not actually have to care about her future husband? She had always said, in her mind, that she would be a good wife, but had defined that as a person who worked hard, stayed quiet and perhaps produced children. Now, she began to think that she wanted to be more than that, more than just a person who stayed out of Jeff's way. She wanted to make Jeff happy, to help him to feel fulfilled in his life. She began to wish that she could make him feel loved. That's what he deserved, but she didn't imagine that was something she could ever give him. The hard truth was that if she really loved him, she must give him what he wanted, what would make him truly happy: a life without a wife. Every time the idea arose in her restless mind, though, she shook it away or stomped it into oblivion. What was done was done.

***

Jeffrey tried his level-best to enjoy his alone time, just as Susannah had suggested. He had always planned a solitary life. Conqueror of his own proud world, he would be. He had dreamed that life up, in every detail, and worked hard for years to obtain it, but now, he felt very far from the boy who had made those plans. His sleep out in the open range each night, as he traveled, was not filled with the peace he had imagined in his youth. It was marred by Susannah's absence on the blanket beside him. He missed her scent, her warmth and the sound of her breathing. Each long day of riding felt so different without knowing he would see her at the end of it. This was exactly the kind of thing he had always planned on doing with his time, and yet he was bored, and for the first time in his life, lonely.

Loneliness, he discovered, was very different from solitude. He tried to while away the hours by considering his future plans for his ranch. He thought about how he still needed to build a larger corral wrapped around the barn with a squeeze chute and attached holding pens. Musings like this used to thrill him and make him feel happy, but without his wife to talk to, his ideas felt a little flatter than they used to. He longed for Susannah's voice in conversation and for the way he usually piled up all the little thoughts and occurrences of the day to tell her later. What had happened to him? This did not used to be the way his mind worked. His habits had changed, along with his feelings and thought patterns. He couldn't sort it all out. It was like he didn't know himself anymore.

Each night, he slept restlessly, examining thoughts and feelings that had never entered his mind before, and each morning he woke up confused and not looking forward to anything. Each day, he rode a little harder and longer, determined to get this trip over with and get back to his wife as fast as possible, and totally shocked that he, the man who had angrily insisted that he never wanted a wife, had become someone who could even consider such a thing as hurrying back to her.

He missed Susannah. He missed her like he had never missed anything in his life. He missed her with a level of intensity he hadn't even known was possible in the realm of missing people. He missed her so much that he didn't even want to fight it, or argue with it, or deny it. He just wanted to be with her again and was resolved to get done with his task quickly and get home.

Chapter 14

Jeffrey's arrival back home was like a sparkling clear sky that comes before a dark and brooding storm.

With effort, Jeff managed to turn the two week trip into twelve days and surprised his wife in the middle of hanging wet laundry on the line. She sensed a disturbance in the quiet world around her and turned to see her husband approaching in the distance. He was riding Merriment, whose back and sides were packed with parcels and bags, and leading a small dairy cow down the slope of the big hill to the east. Susannah's reaction was visceral. Her whole body filled with sudden excitement, desire and pure unleashed joy. Without her command, her legs burst into a full-fledged run. For the first hundred yards, Susie's mind kept chanting that the man she loved was home, home, home, but as the seconds stretched out, her heart began to settle as her long skirt tangled around her ankles. The prairie brush snatched at her and the cold, late afternoon wind blew hard across her face, waking her from her initial dreamy reaction and bringing her back to reality. Yes, her mind suddenly remembered, the man she loved was home, but he was the man who did not love her back. The man she had wronged.

Susannah stopped in her tracks. Her eyes smarted with unexpected tears and she raised her apron to wipe them away. She glanced around aimlessly, feeling suddenly disoriented. Jeffrey was a kind man, she reminded herself, but he had never wanted a wife and certainly did not need her rushing into his arms. No, she must be useful and calm. She gulped several breaths of air, settling her panting lungs and her stampeding heartbeats.

By the time Jeff finally made it to his wife's side, she was quiet and serene, standing like a poem in the midst of swaying prairie grass. The early autumn breezes melted her clothing against her young body and blew her skirt and apron strings outward toward the west. Her auburn locks were loosened just a little, releasing wispy tendrils of dark scarlet to caress her face. She stared at him with eyes full of glow and mystery. He could not read what she was thinking and, although he had imagined this moment a hundred times already, he suddenly did not know how to approach her.

Susannah stood looking up at Jeff as he drew near on horseback, only a few paces away. He looked more handsome than he had ever looked before. The late sunlight glinted off his rich brown hair and his cheeks were ruddy with travel and wind. The way his gaze washed over her made her feel strange and confused. He slipped down off his horse so fast, she almost missed the movement.

Jeff's body proceeded forward without him. His eyes never left Susannah's face. His foot was down out of the stirrup and hitting the ground before the horse had even stopped moving. His steps carried him toward his wife, standing there as she was, in the middle of the wide open prairie in front of their house. No painter could have captured the deep beauty of his home, the way it looked with Susannah standing so still in the open meadow with the cabin and forest framed so perfectly behind her. He wanted to leave her motionless there forever, and at the same time he wanted to pick her slender form up off its feet and twirl her like a school girl. His breath caught. His mind suddenly shut down and he froze.

The two of them stood, just a few feet apart, staring silently at each other. Then gradually, and suddenly, as if those two speeds could happen at the same moment, all Susannah's miserable dark feelings over the mistakes she felt she had made, and her sorrows at ruining Jeff's life, were all overwhelmed, by far, by her incredible joy to see him again. That powerful feeling broke through the others like a sunbeam bursting through the clouds. Completely against her will, she smiled so bright, and so fiercely, that Jeff couldn't help but respond with an equally vivid grin, which, of course, changed his face so completely that it stole Susie's breath away. Her mouth dropped open at the sheer intensity of her attraction to him. It was like a punch in the gut. Her arms opened involuntarily and he jumped forward and hugged her tight, lifting her off the ground and squeezing her with such warmth that she knew she would carry the feeling with her forever.

"It's so good to see you smile, Susie," he whispered in her ear. "So, so good." He released her reluctantly, and stepped back, feeling awkward all of the sudden. He cleared his throat. "Um....I.....missed you."

When Jeff set her down and let go of her, Susannah regained her mental and physical footing. She did not believe his words. He couldn't have missed someone he had never even wanted around. He was just saying and doing what he thought were the customary things to say and do after an absence. She took another fortifying breath of cool clear air and forced her mind and body to calm down. She spoke softly and carefully, though her limbs still quivered with odd sensations. "That's kind of you to say."

"It's true, Susannah," Jeff reached for her hand. "I never missed anything like I missed you."

"Well," she responded, still not believing him, "I missed you too." She put her hand on the side of his face. "So much." She blinked. Her control had slipped. She withdrew her hand and glared at it like it was a traitor. Another breath shuddered through her, helping her. She could not stand there anymore. Inside, Jeffrey probably wanted to be done with greeting his unwanted bride and move on to his ranch tasks, she reminded herself. She must help him. "So, this is our cow." She moved away and took hold of the rope that tied the cow to Merriment's saddle. "I promise, I'll make good butter and keep good track of all the milking and so on...." She glanced back at Jeff, humbly. "Whatever you need me to do, Jeff."

Jeffrey's brows came together in confusion and mild frustration. Why was she saying such things? It sounded like that old Susannah from their first days together, before they had gotten to know each other. New concerns and worries filled his mind.

"Susie," he answered, "You take care of the cow however you like. I don't know anything about all the amazing things you can make with her milk." He suddenly perked up. "Hey! Look what else I've brought you." He pulled something from his belt. "They're tougher gloves than those old garden ones you have. They'll protect your hands when you're working with wood and tools and so on..and...and...lookie here—" He bounded forward like a school boy, "I can't wait to show you!"

Holding the thick gloves, Susie was thankful to be distracted from her inner struggle for a moment, and overwhelmed with Jeff's thoughtfulness. She directed her eyes to where Jeff was headed and noticed that the saddle bag near her was pinned open to let plenty of light and air in. Jeff reached inside and scooped something out. She stared at his hand as it slowly opened. There in the palm of his riding glove, was a soft yellow chick. Susannah gasped at the cute, peeping surprise. Automatically, the new gloves slid into her apron pocket and she reached out to hold the tiny animal.

"Oh, Jeff, Oh!" She grinned. "He's so cute!"

Jeff hesitated, thrilled to see another smile on Susannah's face. He had hoped his gifts would have this effect and it appeared that his efforts had paid off. It felt good to be right. Susie had not lost her smile forever, after all. Finally, he snapped out of his frozen stance and tore his eyes away from his wife's face. He dipped both hands into the saddlebag and pulled out more chicks.

"We're going to have chickens, Susannah!" He cuddled two baby chicks against his chest as Susannah gently rubbed one of the downy little balls of fluff along her cheek. "We'll keep them inside for the winter, since they're so little and don't have a mother hen to keep them warm, but first thing this spring, I'm going to put up a nice coop for them." He petted a new chick he pulled from the bag. "I got them from several different broods, so they should reproduce well. Come March, you'll have eggs regular, and your food is already so amazing that I can't even imagine the masterpieces you'll whip up when you add eggs to your ingredient list and chicken meat too."

Three little chicks peeped as Susannah snuggled them in the crook of her neck. "And their droppings are so good for the garden. Oh, thank you Jeff!"

The world grew quiet again and Jeffrey and Susannah, their hands full of yellow bits of life, and their hearts heavy with mixed-up feelings, slowly ambled along to the barn, pulling the horse and cow behind them.

***

The warm fuzzy chicks settled into a crate in the corner of the cabin just as the warm fuzzy feelings of Jeffrey's return settled and dissipated in Susannah's heart. The sunny bright excitement, when Jeff first arrived, gave way to the old storms of doubt and self-loathing that had been churning inside her for many weeks. The brooding tempest came after the brief sparkle of happy sky.

Her days were filled with more work than ever, as she began to get ready for winter, but the canning, preserving, sewing, knitting, milking, churning, cooking, laundering and other endless tasks, could not fill the holes inside her. It was like her happiness had been shot through with bullets of shame and remorse and she fired new volleys at herself each day. She tried to pray and be thankful. She tried to be quiet and useful, but her love for Jeff was growing more and more as time went by, and with it her guilt.

One day, a week before Thanksgiving, Susannah put on her scarf and headed off into the crisp forest. Her occasional visits to forage in the woods were the only thing that helped quiet her mind and gave her a brief break from the awful clarity and brightness of her glaring thoughts out in the sunshine. There was something soothing about the dark of the woods. It was like hiding, like tamping down her feelings with the weight of branches and shadows.

She marveled at the endless shades of fire around her. The trees had given their lush greens over to gingers, crimsons and sunny vivid golds. Her journey was accompanied by the autumn music of forest sounds. Rare southern chipmunks skittered nearby, cold wind battered the branches above and dry dropped leaves crinkled and crunched beneath her shoes.

Susannah was thinking of her friend Ashley Anderson. They had had such a lovely time together on their two visits, once back at the Anderson Ranch, when the newlyweds had first arrived, and again when the whole Anderson family, and their ranch hands, had traveled over and, so generously, helped the Bridges build their barn. Ashley had introduced her new neighbor to the scarce and elusive sand cherries that grew sparsely across the west. Susie had never seen them where she lived in Kansas. Their flavor was extremely tart, but they were Jeffrey's favorite and even though they were months past their best ripeness, Susannah was determined to find some and make them into a pie for her husband for Thanksgiving. Even if the sour, purple-black fruits might be all shriveled when she located them, Susie had needed a walk in the woods very much, and she knew she could plump the berries back up with hot water and plenty of sugar. So, she breathed in the brisk fall air, and the intoxicating smells of the forest, and tried to let go of some of the tension that her constantly distraught mind had forced into her muscles.

At mid-summer, when the hard-to-find sand cherries had reached their perfect ripeness, Susannah had discovered a small grove of the sun-loving little trees growing in a cheery open clearing. She searched for the spot now, picking up her skirts and wading through undergrowth, as her eyes scanned ahead for the break in branch cover over the little lost meadow. She wished she had marked the way somehow, for she had only seen her destination once, months ago, and it was beginning to seem that she had been walking for far too long. Her mind wandered back and forth from its customary gloomy shame, to thoughts of what her cousin Elsie might be doing for Thanksgiving in her new husband's home, to memories of what Ashley had told her of her own November plans, to reorganizing the two-person feast Susie herself was devising for next week. Finally, she thought she spied an opening in the yellow-garbed branches a ways ahead.

She took a step forward and suddenly felt mysteriously unsteady. It was a very odd sensation and her mind could not quite grasp it. She stumbled a few more footfalls, as the leaf-covered ground shuddered and trembled beneath her. Susannah froze like a statue, fear stabbing her right to the core. Before she could even think to flee or scream, the earth beneath her gave way in a rumbling crash that seemed far quieter than it should have been. Her feet went out from under her, and she felt herself falling. Wood struck her, and dirt and debris flew against her body. Her arms scrambled and scratched for a hold on something, anything.

It was only a moment before Susannah's flailing body settled, but it felt like a slow nightmare. Bruised and spluttering, Susannah coughed away the dirt and leaves that covered her face. Her arms were strained as she hung by them. Rubbing her face against her shoulder, she managed to clear her eyes enough to look up and see that her hands were clinging to a large root that was sticking out of the ground, but there was something foreign about what she was seeing. It took her a few seconds to identify what was disorienting her. The root was shooting sideways out of sideways ground. Sideways ground? Her mind fumbled and she fought panic. She took stock of her body and the different sensations she felt in it: aches, scrapes, feet hanging, arms pulled tight with weight. She was definitely upright. Her legs were down and her hands were up, higher than her head. It was like she was standing up straight, except her feet weren't actually standing on anything, just dangling in thin air. So, how was it possible for the ground to be parallel with her body if she was not lying down?

Susannah didn't yet understand what had happened, but she knew, somehow, that she must not let go. Jiggling more dirt off of her face by vigorously shaking her head back and forth, she suddenly felt her body swinging. Her feet clambered for a hold and found some kind of small outcropping. Her legs relaxed and she felt stable, at least physically. The intense pull on her arms eased. She leaned her forehead against the sandy dirt and took several long breaths as her stomach did flip flops inside her. Finally, she gathered herself enough to start figuring out where she was.

Bravely, tentatively, Susie tilted her head away from her arms and looked around. The early afternoon sun was streaming down through a new gap in the forest cover above and she could see clearly, but it wasn't a gap, it was a breach. Somehow the trees that had been there, blocking the sky, had been ripped away, violently and abruptly. Upward, Susannah could see the woods over her head, on top of at least ten feet of raw dirt, as freshly turned as if a shovel had opened it to the air. Around her was a gaping uneven hole in the ground about as big as the cabin. Below, Susannah could see a jumble of what used to be above. There were whole trees, broken and tangled and very far down, some of which were mired in mud and water. She estimated it was a drop of at least fifty or sixty feet.

Susannah squeezed her eyes shut. She had a sudden memory of her father taking her on a walk, when she was a child, and showing her a sunken place in the back field where underground water had loosened and worn away the hidden places under their feet until the thin layer of surface could no longer hold itself up. Eventually such places collapsed under their own weight.

"A sinkhole," Susannah whispered to herself. "I've fallen into a sinkhole."

Susannah did not entertain the initial shouting inside her mind of: How could this happen? Why me? What are the odds? I was just walking along! Instead, fear overwhelmed all thinking and she started to climb without any careful consideration. The ground her skirt-tangled shoes grasped for, crumbled beneath her attacks, and the root that was her lifeline slid deeper down the side of the chasm. Susannah let out her first scream, dug her feet into a new ledge and forced her body into perfect stillness. She blinked back tears of terror and tried to stop herself from hyperventilating. Climbing was out of the question. The soft side of the sinkhole would give way if she moved, and the bottom was too far down to survive the fall, at least not without many broken bones. She pictured her body slamming and bending against the chunks of wood and jutting up tree-limbs, like a rag doll thrown into a briar patch. If she slipped, she'd be battered to death or skewered like meat on a fork.

Susannah pressed herself tighter into the dirt wall and tried to think. Slowly, her heart calmed down and her mind cleared. She realized that if she couldn't get herself out, then she must find a way to call for help. Jeffrey was too far away to hear her cries, but maybe he could hear a gunshot. Susannah slowly jiggled her hips, feeling for the hard metal of her new pistol against her dress. It wasn't there. Jeffrey had brought her a used revolver from his trip to town. He had shown her how to clean it, load it and fire it. She had fashioned a simple waist holster for the small gun and found it much easier to carry around than the rifle because it wasn't always bouncing against her back and getting in her way when she leaned over. She had strapped the hand gun on before her walk into the woods, in case she ran into a wolf or some other dangerous animal. Susannah squeezed her eyes shut again. Shame washed over her, a familiar feeling by now. She had lost Jeffrey's new gun. Once again, she was a hindrance to his life.

Jeffrey. Her mind filled with images of his face. He would get home and she wouldn't be there. He would have to come and find her. It would be dark before he made it out this far and he would be hungry and worried. Her mind tumbled over all her failures of the past three months. First, Duckling's injury, then the fire, and now this pointless disaster. Jeffrey had been right from day one. She was nothing but a burden to his beautiful life out here on the range. She had spent the spring, and most of the summer, trying to prove to him that having her in his home was good thing, but all she had succeeded in doing was proving to herself that the opposite was true.

This latest calamity was her final lesson in a long awful learning experience. This was it! How much more obvious could the message be? Falling into a sinkhole! It was like being slapped in the face. She could no longer deny what, deep down, she had always known she needed to do. This was a wake-up call, telling her to stop selfishly fighting what was right. She was not supposed to be here. She was not good for Jeffrey. She never would be. She slowed him down, got in his way and made extra work for him. She had brought only adversity and catastrophe to her husband's life. She had been hiding from this truth for weeks, but hanging from a slippery tree root for dear life, she finally accepted it.

Susannah could no longer pretend that she didn't know how to solve this gigantic problem she had created, and undo the harm she had caused. Of course, she knew. She always had. Jeffrey had presented the solution in the very beginning, and she just hadn't cared about him enough to do what he wanted, but that had changed. She had changed, even in such a short time. She thought things now that she never thought she'd think and felt things that she never thought she'd feel. What mattered most had shifted. She was altered beyond her ability to define. She loved Jeff and she couldn't be selfish anymore when she loved him so much. She finally felt ready to give him his life back.

She opened her eyes and stared at the deep hole below her, watching the ripples of destructive water in between splintered logs. Everything grew very quiet, as Susie let the thought come that she had been fighting. She considered the words clearly in her head, one by one, without shoving them away, as she had been doing for so long. A. Long. Distance. Marriage. Her eyes slammed shut, but she shook her head and forced them open again. Yes, she declared inside her heart and mind, yes, she could do it. Yes, she *would* do it! It was the only right thing to do and she was ready to do it now.

An unexpected peace washed over Susannah. Strained muscles relaxed. Dark emotions, trapped in her heart, turned to light, wedging themselves free and vanishing. A weight she had not realized had been nearly paralyzing her, suddenly lifted off and floated away. She breathed clearer than she had in months. The choice was made, and it felt surprisingly good. No more guilt. No more doubts. All would be well now. All would be better and Jeffrey would have his dreams back. Susannah smiled and ignored the tears rolling down her cheeks. They didn't matter. They were for herself, for her own impending loneliness that would soon come with this decision.

Susannah let several minutes roll by quietly, as her new reality sank down into her, like the ground had sunk down into its own new home. This part of the forest was new and changed and so was Susannah. She hung there, suspended physically as she was emotionally, waiting for her life to settle, as the dirt had settled around her. It was a powerful process. She felt free, but smaller. She breathed deeply, as the shadows shifted in the trees and fresh shafts of late sunshine rained down on her. Finally, she felt settled enough to start designing a plan. She had hours before Jeffrey would find her. She had time to find a way to make this new trajectory for her life work somehow.

Riding, she could reach the nearest town herself, in less than a week, just like Jeffrey had done recently, but there would be no way to return Jeff's horse to him and she didn't want to take one of his mounts away from the ranch for so long anyway. What if she walked? Even if she didn't get lost, that would probably take over a month. The snows would come. She'd never make it, but she did not trust her resolve to last until spring. She needed to get this over with. Again, Susie's thoughts went to Ashley. Of course! The Andersons could get her away from Jeffrey's ranch. Susannah's mind whirred, examining every detail.

Her friend had told her that every year the Anderson family traveled three days south to a relative's house for Thanksgiving, then three days north to North Platte for winter supplies, before heading back home. They arrived safe and sound, back at their little ranch, in early December, beating the first snows. On horseback, Ashley and Christopher's ranch was less than a day's ride. If she made it to them before they left on their trip, Jeff's horse could be returned, and she was sure her friends would be happy to take her along. Once she reached North Platte, she would simply catch a stagecoach.

Susannah had some money tucked away, in the lining of her carpet bag, that had been there ever since her old neighbors had sold all her parents' belongings to buy her a stage ticket when she was ten. A nice lady had given her a loaf of bread to eat, on the short three day journey, and sewn the rest of the money into the bag. Susie had never touched it, knowing someday a need would arise. This was that day. It was enough cash to buy a canteen for water and a three hundred mile ticket on one of the cheaper stage lines.

Hopefully, there would be a few coins leftover for a little food along the way to supplement whatever she could take with her. Most way stations provided a quick stretch of the legs to the privy and a gulped cup of coffee, while the horses were changed out, but a few provided food for purchase that you could grab and eat on the way. Susannah had learned when traveling as a child, that most stagecoaches, especially ones like the cut-rate, low-quality one she would have to find, slowed down for nothing, not for sleep, not for meals, not for little kids who are still in the outhouse. Winter never delayed a greedy stagecoach company, and it was early still, as far as the coming cold was concerned. A few flurries here and there were nothing to worry about. Susannah had her scarf and her warm hand-me-down cloak. With extra horses and less weight, stagecoaches were faster than covered wagons by far. Traveling day and night, whenever possible, and stopping only for those brief way station pauses to change out the team, a good stagecoach driver could have Susie near her hometown in, maybe, a little over a week. Coaches didn't run through a little nothing place like Seagleton, but nearby Collingsworth or even Dodge City would do. She could make it the rest of the way in the back of some kindly traveler's wagon. She'd remember to save a coin or two to pay that person.

So, Susannah nodded to herself, ignoring the ache in her fingers as she gripped the root, it was doable. She'd be fine. She'd be back with her aunt and uncle before the ground froze and the heavy snows came. She'd be shivering under her old quilt, in no time, in that barn she'd hoped she'd never see again. She shook away negative thoughts and tried to focus on something lighter, like getting home in time to share Christmas with her little cousins.

The sunshine, through the new tear in the tree cover, was growing dimmer, little by little, as the day dragged on. Jeffrey would not be much longer, just a few hours. As she waited, hanging over the sheer drop that she refused to look at again, Susannah turned her thoughts to all the little details that needed to fall into place to set her plan into motion. She would make a batch of molasses cookies to contribute to the Thanksgiving Dinner she was inviting herself to. They would keep for days, stuffed in her carpet bag. She would rise early and make lots of food to last Jeffrey a while. It wasn't like she was going to sleep a wink tonight, anyway. She would have to ask one of the Anderson ranch hands to take Jeff's horse back to him. In her mind, she ran over each man she remembered from the barn raising, picking out the most trustworthy one. On and on, her mind twirled, spinning every detail into perfect order. By the time Jeffrey found Susannah, she was calm, collected and resolved.

Chapter 15

Jeff arrived home just before dusk, tired, but feeling good about how much work he had gotten done on the fencing. After the coming snows cleared, he thought he might concentrate on building a bunkhouse for his ranch hands. He would hire them first, sometime in late February, and by the end of March, they'd have the bunkhouse up and be well on the way to finishing the endless fences around his property. He nodded his head with satisfaction at his plans, as he dismounted, pulled his rifle from its slot on the side of his saddle and set it against the wall. Then, noticing the new cow mooing, he removed the saddle, led Ducky into her stall and took off her bridle. He bent down to examine her leg and smiled to see that it was impossible to tell that there had ever been an injury. Ducky was strong and happy. She seemed no worse for wear. He heard a noise and spoke out.

"Yep, Duckling has made a full recovery," he said, standing up. "A day of work didn't bother her at all."

Stepping out of the stall and latching Ducky's door, Jeff smiled and turned to see his wife's expression. She wasn't there. His face fell and his eyebrows furrowed in confusion. It must have been some other sound he had heard and he had just assumed it was Susie's approach. She always came to the barn by now, when he was coming in for the night. Always, without fail. She watched for him at the window as she prepared supper. With the flat ground on the other side of the stream, she could see his approach for quite a while before he arrived. It was odd for her not to be here yet. Perhaps she was stirring something or taking something off the fire. Surely, she would arrive in a moment.

The cow that Susannah had named "Custard", after the first dish she had made with the new milk, was still lowing loudly. Momentarily distracted from his thoughts of Susie's absence, he went to check on the uncomfortable animal. Grabbing a pail, he released a few streams of milk from the cow's tight udders until Custard relaxed with relief. Jeff frowned. Quickly, he finished the milking. What could have kept Susie from milking the cow in the late afternoon like she always did?

Suddenly concerned, Jeff closed the cow in her stall and exited the barn quickly. He stood with his hands on his hips, staring at the cabin across the farmyard. There was no movement near his house. He looked around. The stream was gurgling along. The sun was setting slowly across the prairie behind him, filling the sky with creamy roses and pale lavenders. The cold autumn wind brushed back and forth through the tall grasses like it was chasing something. Merriment stomped her hoof inside the corral. The kitchen garden's branch fence rattled a little, buffeted by the evening breezes, and all else was still and silent, broken only by the soft cries of ground sparrows as they settled down in the undergrowth to sleep. Jeff's eyes swept his yard again, listening. Something did not feel right.

Turning back to grab the rifle, he broke into a jog, rushed over to the cabin and pulled on the string at the entrance. The bar lifted and the front door swung inward. Jeff's mouth fell open. No lanterns or candles were lit. No supper was laid. The cooking had not even been started. In fact, the fire had gone out. The chicks peeped emphatically from their enclosure in the corner. They never did that at this time of day, because Susie fed them right before he got home and they would have full tummies and be happy little creatures calming down for the night, but not this night. She had not fed them. Fear clenched Jeffrey's heart. He ran out of the house, slipping the rifle strap over his head and shoulder as he went, and not even closing the door behind him.

Jeff rushed down the woodsy path to the outhouse, and when he did not find Susannah there, he doubled over in panic. Bending at the waist, he placed his hands on his thighs and stared at the ground. He tried to calm his breathing. "Susannah!!" he called, standing up again. "Susannah!!" He waited. There was no response.

Jeffrey raced back to the house at a full run. He glanced at the corner where Susie kept her baskets, as he shoved some matches into his pocket. His wife's foraging basket was gone and her pistol holster was not on its peg. He grabbed a lantern and took off towards the woods, this time barely pausing long enough to make sure the door was closed. Susie had to be in the forest. She went there regularly to check traps and gather things like flowers, honey, herbs and berries. It was the only logical explanation that he wanted to even consider. All other possibilities conjured up far worse ideas than he could handle. Jeff did not know which direction Susannah had gone, so, he sort of aimed at the middle of the expanse of trees behind the cabin and crashed right in, roughly disturbing bushes and trampling vegetation loudly as he went.

Deeper and deeper, he clambered through the woods at a fast speed, the rifle slapping against his back with every step. He narrowly avoided getting hit by branches. Every few minutes, he stopped and called his wife's name, but there was no response. Either she was very far away, or she couldn't hear him. He didn't want to think about why she might not be able to hear him. He looked for signs of her passage through the trees, but could see little of anything in the deep purple light descending through the branches as the sun set. After what felt like about half an hour, Jeffrey ran smack into a tree and finally stopped, realizing that at some point the dim murkiness of dusk had turned to sheer black. He couldn't see his hand in front of his face. He forced himself to be still enough to strike a match on the same tree that had attacked him and light the lantern. He sighed. Carrying a flame would slow him down. If he rushed too much and swung the lantern too violently, the flicker of fire inside would go out. He took a deep breath and walked on more carefully, but it took all his willpower not to run.

An hour of darkness had passed when Jeffrey started to hear wolves howling in the distance. He imagined all kinds of terrifying fates that could have befallen Susannah. He shoved each one aside, refusing to consider them. His heart pounded. It felt like it was going to break. He could not bear to lose Susannah.

Jeff's thoughts were filled with his wife, as his voice continually shouted her name, and his body carried him on and on through the dark woods. He realized he had never met anyone so kind. He hadn't known it was possible to be so forgiving and patient and strong at the same time, as she was. He was plagued by images of her-- her lovely deep red hair splayed on the pillow beside him, her eyes gleaming with light as she looked at him, her little heart-shaped face smiling with a beauty that took his breath away. He couldn't imagine the pain if something happened to Susie. Somewhere along the way, Jeffrey had gotten used to her. Used to her gentle ways, her soft voice, her woman's touches on his home that made everything better. She made his life full when it would have been empty. He'd grown to look forward to seeing her after hours of hard work, and he actually liked to find out what she had been doing each day and what little triumphs she had accomplished. He enjoyed sharing his thoughts and ideas with her and hearing her contributions to his plans, something he never ever expected to find any pleasure in, but he did. Slowly, he had begun to wonder what it would be like to sleep with his arms around her, instead of lying pulled away and pressed into the wall. Jeffrey had started to imagine a future filled with her influence on his ranch and on his heart. He had been almost ready to admit his feelings to himself, during that agonizing trip to town without her, when missing her had ached so intensely. Now, he fought the same battles in his head again. He had never wanted a wife. Wives were hardship and frustration. That is what he had long believed and planned for, but Susie was not just any wife, she was Susie. She had somehow become a part of him and crept her way into his world, leaving her handprints everywhere, and altering his goals. He had different dreams now, but he still couldn't quite put into words what it all meant. He had never been good at defining his emotions. All he knew, right now, was that he absolutely had to find her and she had to be alive. He could not stand to go home without her. It wouldn't be home anymore.

He stopped again. "Susie-e-e-e!!" he called out, at the top of his lungs. "Susannah! Susannah, where are you-ou-ou…?" He dragged his words out, willing them to spread and echo and penetrate the thickness of the forest. He closed his lips and waited, straining his ears for a response. Just as he picked his foot up to continue forward, he thought he heard something. Something faint, but human.

"Susie??" He yelled, turning towards the noise.

"Jjjjfff…vrrr…hee..rrr…" The muffled tones reverberated off the trees.

He had definitely heard something that time. "I hear you!" he shouted, and ran another ten yards in the direction of the voice, stomping over bushes and shoving tree limbs out of his way with his free hand. Then, he stopped again to listen. "Susie, where are you? Keep calling out!"

"Jeff! Jeff!" Susie's voice broke into the silent darkness, quiet and far, but clear. "I'm over here! I'm over here!"

"I'm coming!" Jeff cried and burst into full speed, running towards his wife's voice. It was suddenly the best sound he'd ever heard.

"Over here!"

Jeff stopped so abruptly that he almost tripped. He squinted his eyes, holding the lantern out at arm's length, desperately trying to see. That last cry had come from very close. She was here somewhere. Why couldn't he see her? Why didn't she run to him?

"Susie, I'm here, but I....I don't see you."

"Be careful, Jeff. I'm below you." Susie's voice was no longer yelling. She was close enough to speak to at a regular volume, but he still did not see her. "Look down," she continued, "But don't get too close."

Jeff searched all around him, staring at the ground and turning in circles. He took a few steps forward until the lantern's circle of light finally revealed a crumbly edge and a swath of strange darkness. He froze again, looking up and down. The moonlight wafted earthward, through a break in the tree cover, over what seemed like some kind of giant gash in the forest floor. His eyes adjusted and his mind caught up. Susie was down inside some sort of chasm!

"No!" Jeff threw himself onto his stomach and edged carefully toward the lip of the broken ground. "Susie?" His fingers reached the hole and dirt disintegrated beneath them.

"Careful!" Susie yelped, as the soil rained down on her. "It will collapse."

Jeff's head finally pulled slowly over the edge of the hole. He carefully lifted his lantern out in front of him. It hung in open air, illuminating a cavity in the ground as big as his house and deeper than the trees were tall. His wife hung from the side below him, further away than his arms could reach.

"Susie, what!" He glanced around frantically, swinging the lantern. "What happened?"

"It's a sinkhole," she said calmly. "I'm ok."

"You...you...," he fumbled, scared. "I....I'll get you out."

Jeff sat up slowly, not wanting to cave in the unstable ground below his knees. He mentally slapped himself for not bringing a rope. He swung the lantern again, arcing swirls of butter yellow light around him, trying to find something to help his wife. Setting the lantern in between two strong roots jutting out along the ground, he strained to reach a long branch nearby without shifting his weight. He pulled it close and tested its strength. It was pretty long, long enough to be heavy in his hands. It stuck out away from him too far to see the end of it in the small dome of lantern glow. He broke off several weak twigs at the end, leaving only a few strong protrusions and the thick core of the three bough, which was wider than two or three arms put together and should hold Susie's weight without breaking. He was worried about her fingers being able to hold on. They had to be numb from grasping tightly for hours on the side of that sinkhole. She could probably barely feel her hands. He could not be certain that she would not slip right off the branch if she tried to grip it. Thinking fast, he removed his belt and refastened it back into a circle. Then he entwined it through two big offshoots that forked off the sides of the center branch. He pulled hard on the belt and it did not come loose.

"Here, see if this limb will reach you," he said, lowering the branch cautiously. From his angle, positioned to pull, he could not see Susannah. He listened for her answer.

"I can feel it," she said. "It's long enough."

"Ok, now carefully slide my belt over both your arms so it holds you under your shoulders. Understand?"

"Yeah," Susie responded.

She could not feel her hands, but she could still control them. Very very slowly, she released one hand without shifting her body at all. Her fingers were cold and lifeless. She could not make them grasp the belt. Gently, she moved her arm down to rest along the side of her skirt, with her deadened fingers against her thigh. With a trickle of warmth, the blood began to run painfully back into her hand. She waited, wiggling her fingers until she could feel them. Then she swung her arm back up, slid it inside the circle of the belt and grabbed tightly onto the branch. Step by step, she repeated the same motions with her other arm until both her hands were clutching the large branch and the belt was securely wrapped around her upper back and digging into her armpits. She had not lost her balance and did not relish the thought of giving up her toehold on the soft dirt wall, but she took a long deep breath and steeled herself to be brave.

"Ok," she said, a little shakily. "I'm ready."

"Are you sure?" Jeff called, more frightened than he had ever felt in his life. "You…uh…you say when, only….only if you're sure…"

"I'm sure, Jeffrey," Susannah's voice called out, soft and clear and filled with sweetness. She was actually trying to comfort him while she dangled over a sheer black abyss. He blinked, breathing in several times, preparing himself. "It's ok, Jeff," Susie said. "It's ok, pull me up."

Jeff needed to be as brave as his wife. He gathered his courage and smashed away mental images of her falling. He positioned his feet under him in a squat, gripped the branch and pulled. As the long bough moved, with Susannah's weight palpable on the end of it, Jeff slowly but steadily took a few footfalls back and moved upwards until he was standing. He kept pulling, stumbling backwards, until he felt Susie's angle change from straight down to sideways. She had come up over the lip, like a fish being pulled into the boat for supper. He kept going, dragging her several feet away from the edge, back onto solid ground that would not dissolve beneath her. Jeff could see Susie's ruby-chestnut hair, disheveled and shining in the dim light of the lantern which was now many steps away from him. He dropped the branch and ran forward, scooping her up before she could even move.

Jeffrey tore the wood and leather away from Susannah and gathered his wife into his lap. She felt solid and yet fragile and small in his arms. She did not seem half as upset as he was. He was actually blinking back a few tears, something that had never happened to him before, not since childhood. His heart was racing and trying to pound its way right out of his chest, but Susannah was breathing slowly and calmly. Her arms went around his shoulders as she rested against him, her head nestled beneath his chin. She patted him on the back in a rhythmic soothing pattern.

"It's ok, now," she whispered, pulling herself up so her mouth was beside his ear. He could smell the dirt in her hair. "It's ok. I'm ok. I'm sorry this happened, but we're ok, now. Nothing to fret about. It's all ok, now."

Her voice sounded odd. The kindness was hers, but something else in her tone just didn't sound like her. Jeff was so disturbed by this whole experience that he could barely speak. He wanted to say so much and had no idea how to say any of it, so he said nothing. He could feel that his silence was a mistake, but he couldn't make his throat unclench.

Susannah pulled away without showing her reluctance to do so. She would have preferred to stay in Jeff's embrace forever, but her determination was set on a new course and she must not waver from the decision she had made while in that hole. She had to unbend Jeff's fingers from her hair and pry his other hand from around her waist, but she finally managed to stand. He remained on the ground, staring up at her, feeling lost. She leaned a little from side to side, then forward and back, stretching the aches out of her body. She stamped her feet and shook her arms, then tilted her neck around in a circle. He just watched her.

"You....you hurt?" He finally managed to stammer.

"I'm just fine, Jeff." She looked at him, her eyes lowering and coming together in a strange humble scowl. "I...I'm...just sorry this happened. This is all you need in the middle of the night. Why, I bet Custard is just a-wailin' and the little chicks must be cheepin' up a storm, and you must be starving." She bent down and yanked on him until he stood up. "Come, let's get you home." She picked up the lantern and walked away.

Jeffrey was stunned. Get me home, he thought, get me home? Susannah's reaction to this near-death crisis was not normal, but Jeff was so emotionally exhausted, so weary with relief, so utterly confused, that all he could do was turn and follow the bobbing light of the lantern as it floated away towards the ranch.

Chapter 16

Susannah didn't sleep at all that night. She was exhausted and her body ached, but her eyes simply wouldn't close. After eating a cold biscuit, putting Merriment in the barn, and feeding the horses and chickens, Jeff had fallen into a deep slumber, pressed against the wall like always, but this time with his hand holding his wife's. The sensation of his gentle clasp actually seemed to ease the pain in her palm where it still tingled with tender soreness. Jeff had not spoken a word to her since she had headed towards home through the pitch black forest. She stared at his sleeping face in the shadows now, thinking that she deserved no less. She deserved to never hear his voice again. The way he couldn't even speak to her, only further confirmed that her decision to leave him was right. A new fire she had started in the fireplace flickered enough glow around the one-room cabin for her to see her husband's features. So, she lay there listening to him breathe, watching his eyes move beneath his lids as he dreamed, and reveling in the warm feel of his fingers in her own for the last time. After months of feeling completely lost, Susannah could finally see her path in front of her again.

Just an hour after lying down, Susannah rose in the darkness. She had calmly combed the dirt from her hair earlier, and now she pinned it up neatly, pulled out her carpet bag and placed the comb in it. By the light of only one candle, she made several loaves of bread and batches of biscuits. She whipped up bowls of seasoned vegetables, a honeybutter pie, and forty molasses cookies. She tucked all the food away into nooks and shelves while Jeffrey slept like a log. She tiptoed up to the bed and gently lifted her father's Bible from its spot nearby, where she read it each night. She held it to her chest and then slipped it into her bag. Having flashbacks of her time as a heartbroken grieving child, she packed one of the loaves of bread for her journey, just like the time that nice neighbor had given her bread for her very first stagecoach trip. She wrapped the loaf in a towel and buried it deep in her carpet bag, to save for after the eight days of travel and visiting it would take to get to North Platte. She packed her mother's handkerchief and quietly rolled up a few articles of clothing and dropped them in as well, then pushed the bag back under the bed. She swept the whole house and cleaned every shelf and surface as thoroughly as she could in the low light. Finally, she started working on a big hearty breakfast. It would be the only goodbye she would have from Jeff.

By the time Jeffrey awoke, just before sunrise as usual, Susie had milked the cow, fed the chicks and was pulling thick flapjacks off her skillet over the fire. Jeff ran out to the outhouse, and to do his morning chores, and by sunrise he was returning to a table which bore not only the giant flapjacks, but golden hashbrowns, warmed molasses, soft butter, fluffy biscuits, steaming coffee with a bowl of frothy cream, and sweet cinnamon sticky buns drizzled with honey. Susannah sat knitting in the corner, with a pale face she had concealed by pinching her cheeks.

"My, oh, my, Susannah," Jeff said, smiling. "What a feast!"

Susie tied off the last yarn row and held up a finished scarf to survey it briefly, then she rose from her work as Jeff washed his hands. "We needed something nice after last night."

Jeffrey turned, drying his fingers on a towel. "Are you feeling all right? I still can't believe you don't have any injuries."

"I'm just fine," Susie said, softly. A flash of a memory of some large piece of wood bouncing off her side, sparked across her mind. She self-consciously rubbed one hand across slightly bruised ribs and resisted the urge to stretch her throbbing shoulders.

They sat down to eat, but didn't say much during the meal. Suzy couldn't think of anything to say and didn't want to make Jeff suspicious by saying the wrong thing. So, she ate quietly and watched her husband when he wasn't looking, drinking up every detail of him to keep buried in her heart.

Finally, Jeff patted his stomach, mumbled something about having plenty of energy for the day after that meal, dropped his cloth napkin onto his plate and stood up. Susie knew this was her last moment with him and she fought hard to keep her emotions in check. It was very hard. As she ascended slowly from her chair to join him, she blinked a lot and her hands gripped each other until the nails drove into her skin. Jeff didn't notice.

"Well, I guess you do seem as fit as a fiddle, so I'd best get going," Jeff said casually, tilting his head as he looked at her. "Thanks for a great breakfast, Susie-girl."

He stepped out the door with his packed dinner in hand, like always. She followed him to the barn, on the pretense of putting Duckling in the corral for him, so he could get off to work faster, but really she just wanted to stay with him for as long as she could. He stood beside Merriment, who was already saddled, pulled down the stirrup and then turned to look at Susannah. A silent moment passed, as their eyes locked. He sighed and reached out to put his hand on her shoulder, his forefinger swept through the soft hair at the nape of her neck below her auburn bun. Not able to stop herself, she raised both her hands to cover his wrist against her dress, feeling the connection and heat of his strong arm touching her one more time.

She opened and closed her mouth. She couldn't bear not to say something. She finally managed to force her voice to work. "Have a...Have a good time working, Jeff. It's a...," she cleared her throat, somehow managing to conceal a tremble, "It's a beautiful day in this beautiful place you've brought me to, Jeff."

He smiled, pulling his fingers down until his hand caught

between both of hers. "Yes, it is." Almost as beautiful as you, he thought, but could not make his mouth say it out loud. "I… uh..I'm very glad that you're ok, Susie." He smiled at her again and was rewarded by her returning his expression with a sweet quiet smile of her own. Then she let go of his hand and stepped away.

Jeff took his hat from the saddle horn and put it on. He climbed up on Merriment and nudged her with his heels. The horse turned and splashed across the rippling brook. Susannah's hands grasped the sides of her skirt and she arched her neck, watching Jeff's back as he picked up speed. She kept watching, her eyes widening more and more, until he shrank into the distance and disappeared over the horizon. Susie let out a moan, her hands flying to her mouth. She whirled around sharply, turning her back on the vanishing of the man she loved. She squeezed her eyes shut and stamped her foot until she regained control. She would not cry. Not yet. There would be time for that later.

***

Susie threw herself into her preparations, wanting to leave fast, and using the work to keep herself from thinking. She hadn't removed all of her clothes from their pegs because Jeff might have noticed their absence, and she knew from the start that the only way she could do this was by leaving while he was away, without him knowing. Now that he was gone, she tore her winter cloak and remaining dress off the wall and stuffed them in her bag. She rushed around the cabin, setting out all the food she had made on the table where Jeff could easily find it. She draped cheesecloths and towels over everything to keep the bugs away. He would have plenty to eat for a while as he got used to not having someone to cook for him. He'd probably be happy to go back to eating the way he had always planned, she reasoned. She set the scarf she had made on his chair, a present for him.

Finally, Susannah walked over to her kitchen, the western side of the cabin with all her neatly organized jars and bags and dishes and shelves. She ran her fingers over every item one last time and gazed out the window at her garden. She picked up something that had become her most cherished belonging: the wooden spoon that Jeff had carved for her with his own hands. She hugged it close against her chest. She would cherish it forever, and keep it tucked away safe in her loft to remember her husband by. She walked over and carefully slipped it deep inside her carpet bag. Then, sighing, she calmed herself down for the final task, the hardest one.

Slowly, she took a piece of paper to the table and sat with her pencil. She stared for a long moment at the page. She had planned this letter a dozen times as she hung onto the side of that sinkhole last night, but still it was hard to write the words down. There was so much she wanted to say, but couldn't. The letter needed to be simple and direct. All the things she wished she could say were really only for herself. The kind man who had given her her dreams and did not love her, did not need to hear them. Finally, she put the pencil to the paper and began. She wrote:

My dear Jeffrey,

You gave me everything I ever wanted: escape, a new life, a peaceful country home, my little kitchen and garden. You gave me my dreams, but it was at the expense of your own. I got what I wanted, and you got exactly the one thing that you didn't want, and that's not right. For a long time, I told myself that I didn't know how to fix it, but I do, and now that I've grown to love you, I have to give you what will make you happy, because that's what love does. So, I'm going to do what you asked from the beginning. I'm taking Duckling to the Andersons' ranch. They'll return her to you and they'll take me to town where I can catch a stagecoach. We're going to do the long distance marriage, just as you wanted, and I'm actually happier to do it than I would have been before, because I have my memories now, of our home here, and I'll cherish those forever. So, thank you for putting up with an unwanted wife for these lovely six months, so that I could have those wonderful memories to take with me. They will sustain me. I'll be fine now, and I'll be praying for you every night and imagining your full life every day.

I wish you endless happiness,

Your Susie

After writing the letter, Susannah wanted to get out of there. She could feel pain coming and it was going to be bad. She glanced around to be sure she had not forgotten anything. She rushed to a shelf by the bed and grabbed ahold of the blue hairpin that Elsie had given her. She held it and thought of her love for Elsie and the children. She slid the pin into her bag. She could do this. She was strong enough. She had her incredible half-year with Jeffrey, like a treasure inside her, that no one could ever take away, and, just as she had written in the letter, she could live on those memories forever. She had to follow through now, and get far away from here before she broke down and grew weak and changed her mind. This was the hardest thing she had ever done and she must force herself to do it, every step of it, right now. Immediately.

She stuck the corner of the letter under a bowl in the center of the table. Then, leaving the rifle on its hooks above the mantle, she doused the fire with ashes, grabbed her carpet bag and scarf and ran out of the house, slamming the door behind her. She threw a saddle on Duckling, barely taking the time to fasten the girth. She tore the pins from her hair, stuffed them in her pocket and shook her hair loose and free, ready for the ride of her life. Then she looped the handles of her bag over the saddle horn, jammed her foot into the stirrup and swung up in one fast jump. Tapping Ducky's sides with her heels, she grabbed the reins and held on tight as the horse began to trot. She pushed the animal onward into a full run and raced out of the barnyard with the wind blowing through her auburn locks. She squeezed her eyes shut and did not look at the beloved little cabin flying by her.

A moment later, she had reached the tall hill that marked the end of her adored ranch. She and Ducky climbed to the top, and there she finally gathered the courage to say goodbye. Reaching down and patting the golden horse's neck, she swung her around and stared back at the place she loved more than any other spot on earth. Her eyes drank up and memorized every detail: the neat little garden with its country-branch fence, the still new-looking barn rising out of the endless swaying prairie, the bit of woods that had comforted and sheltered her, that stretched into places that were beyond Jeff's property and led to far away waters that she had hoped to see someday, and, last, the precious little cabin that had kept her warm and safe, where she had spent the happiest most fulfilled days of her life. Finally, she dragged her eyes to the most important place, the westward horizon where she had last seen her husband. She pictured him there, far out of sight, becoming more and more a part of this rugged peaceful land, as he worked to make it his own. She breathed one last breath of the crisp clean air of her ranch, her dream home.

"Goodbye, Jeffrey," she whispered, then turned her horse and sped away.

Down the other side of the hill, she flew, pushing Duckling faster and faster until the ranch was miles behind her, then she slowed to an easy canter, for the horse's sake, and looked back to see that her dreams were gone. Her husband and her home were far out of sight and behind her forever.

She had done it and quickly, like tearing a bandage off a wound. That was exactly how Susannah felt. It was as if her determined decision had been holding her together, warding off the painful parts of her choice. Now, she was that bleeding wound, open to the air and unprotected. She let the pain in. Leaving Jeffrey was almost like a death. She would never see him again. She cried and shook with sobs, as Duckling trotted along at a medium clip. The wind slowly dried the saltwater on Susie's cheeks, but she kept drenching them again and again. She let it all out, hour after hour, as she rode further and further away from her dreams and towards her life of lonely oppression. No! She shook herself, after indulging in her grief for long enough. No, her aunt and uncle's house would never be like it was, not ever again. Susannah was different now. She had six months of lovely fulfilling memories to keep her company now and a real living man out there, whose life she could imagine more clearly than those make-believe men she had dreamed up as a kid. As she toiled under Aunt Jane's thumb, she would fill her mind with the joy she had had tending her own garden and running her own kitchen. She would remember the cool quiet stream and the verdant forest softly melting into shocking oranges, scarlets and ambers. When she sat all alone, sewing her fingers to the bone, she wouldn't really be there in that stuffy sitting room. She would be far away, seated at Jeffrey's table, recalling every detail of his voice and laughter, as he told her tales of prairie dog towns, startled jackrabbits and other endless tidbits of life, of which she remembered every one. When seasons changed and her circumstances didn't, Susannah would simply dream of what her dear Jeffrey was doing. Was it time for him to bring in the cows? Was he teaching his ranch hands how to take care of his herd his way, like he always wanted? Was he sleeping sound and safe in the quiet aloneness he had always desired? She would imagine every detail of his life as the years went by, and when she was sweating in the hay-filled barn loft on burning summer nights, or shivering there on frigid mornings, she would curl up under her tattered quilt and pretend it was Jeffrey's arms. She would relive the hugs he had given her at the top and bottom of that beloved hill that led into the place that would always be her home in her heart. She would feel his fingers massaging her shoulders that awkward night by the campfire, and she would drift off every evening into dreams of thankfulness because for one brief half-year, she had had everything she ever wanted. It would be enough. It would have to be. It was far more than many women ever got.

Finally, as the afternoon sunbeams grew long and headed towards the west, Susie, now calm and dry-eyed, arrived at her friends' house. She did not have to explain much, for they welcomed her with open arms and did not ask many questions. Chris said they would be perfectly happy to take her along with them on their journey, and she had made it just in time, as they were leaving tomorrow. After supper, when the young girls were tucked into bed, and Chris and his son had gone out to attend to a few evening chores in preparation for tomorrow's travel, Susie sat with Ashley and poured out her reasons for leaving Jeff. Ashley nodded quietly. Wisdom and non-judgmental gentleness floated in her experienced eyes, as she sewed away on a child's garment. When Susannah finally finished speaking, Ashley sighed and looked right at her.

"Well, my dear," the older woman said, "I can't tell you if you're making a mistake or not. I don't know what's right for your Jeffrey or for you. I always felt that marriage was far better than being alone, but I've never felt unwanted, so I can't tell you what you should do." She stuck the end of her needle through the cloth in two spots to hold her place. "It seems to me that you have thought this through and have made your choice." She settled her unfinished project into her sewing basket. "We'll be happy to have you along for Thanksgiving, Susannah, and we'll see you safely to North Platte. You have nothing to worry about." She stood up and waited for Susie to join her. "I only hope that you don't live a life of regret. If you're not sure, you can change your mind anytime along the way. We'll get you back home again. Won't bother us one bit."

Susannah shook her head. "No, I'm sure. I didn't do this lightly, but I thank you so much for your help and…for your kindness, Ashley."

"No problem, it's what neighbors are for." She put her arm around her friend and led her off to find a bed for the night.

Chapter 17

Jeffrey had a hard day re-living the last night's events. Susannah could have died. He could have searched those woods all night, only to find her body at the bottom of that chasm in the cold light of day. He tried not to picture her broken, bleeding and lifeless. He needed her. He was no longer afraid to admit it and wondered why it had been so hard to do so before. He had been flat out wrong about wives and he was ok with being wrong. Whether a wife was good for a man's home, simply depended on what kind of wife you got and, well, he had definitely gotten a great one. He smiled as he dug another hole for a fence post. He couldn't believe how blessed he had been. Of all the wives he could have ended up with at that fiasco of an arranged wedding, how could he have been so fortunate as to be gifted with his Susannah? Providence. That's all it could be.

Nervous over being away from Susie all day, after what she had been through yesterday, Jeff rushed home at a little faster trot than normal and strained upward in his stirrups as he approached, to try and catch a glimpse of her. When Merriment's hooves sloshed through the stream and Susie still had not come out of the house, his anxiety grew. He waited a moment and there was still no motion at the cabin. This could not be happening again! It couldn't! He nudged the horse and galloped over to the house, hopping to the ground and leaving the horse untethered. Something was wrong. He could feel it, sense it. Something was wrong all over again!

Jeffrey tore the door open and saw the piles of food on the table and the empty spots on the wall where Susannah's second dress and cloak were supposed to be. Noticing the letter, he grabbed it and rushed to the window. Pulling the window covering to the side, to let in the sunset light, he began to read. Susannah's words struck him like daggers. She loved him, the letter said, but she had left him. She was gone. She said she was doing what he had desired from the beginning and she called herself an unwanted wife. That phrase hurt the most. He started to feel physically ill. She wished him a full life and endless happiness, but he knew in his bones that he could never ever have that without her. He wanted to stumble to a chair and sit down, but instead he flew out the door and climbed back on Merriment, who had faithfully waited near the cabin. Without thinking of anything, except that he wanted to catch up to his wife, he raced to the big hill and stopped at the top. Staring out towards the east, he put his hand over his eyes and scanned every rise, every shallow valley between every grassy hill. The sun was setting and Susannah was nowhere to be seen. She probably left long ago. Jeffrey slumped in the saddle and rubbed his face with his riding gloves. How could this happen? What was he going to do? Susie was wrong, so very very wrong. He did want her. He had no wish for a long distance marriage anymore. He nodded to himself, not even surprised at his certainty. He wanted his wife back more than he had ever wanted anything.

Jeff turned and headed back down to the ranch. He put a feedbag of oats over Merriment's head and left her in the barn. He went into the house and poured the chickens enough food for a few days from a jar of scraps and seeds and dead bugs that Susie had set aside for them. He dumped a plate of biscuits into a burlap bag along with some dried meat, grabbed the scarf Susie had made him, noticing that it still smelled like her, and threw his winter coat over his arm. Then he took his rifle down, along with his canteen and headed back out to the barn. He loaded his things onto the horse, milked the cow and tied her to his saddle. He drank some of the warm milk, then took Merri for her own drink at the stream, grateful that he hadn't worked her hard today and didn't need to wait for her to cool down before he fed and watered her. He didn't want anything to delay his pursuit of his bride. Finally, he rode out over the hill and into the eastern prairie at a moderate pace. He was going to reach his Susie.

Jeffrey rode all night long. The moon lit the way and there were no obstacles. When the darkness grew frigid, he put on his coat, wrapped Susie's warm scarf around his neck and kept going. After several hours, he found a large rock and tied the cow there. Custard couldn't make it all the way and he needed to go faster. The sun rose and Merriment grew tired, but Jeff kept going, knowing he was very close to his destination.

Finally, as his eyes began drooping, Jeffrey saw the Anderson house on the horizon. When he made it there, one of the ranch hands greeted him, leading Duckling.

"Hey there, Mr. Bridges, ain't this a surprise," the man said, coming up to Jeff as he dismounted. "I was just about to bring you your horse back, and here you are."

"You look beat, sir," another man said. "Let me get you some coffee." He walked off, but the first man remained, patting Duckling's toffee-colored neck.

"I'm looking for my wife," Jeff declared, stretching his muscles a little as he waited for a response. "Is she here?"

"Sorry, sir," the man holding Ducky's bridle answered. "She left with the boss and his missus a couple of hours ago. They said she was goin' to their Aunt Barbara's house with them for Thanksgiving."

Jeff tore off his hat and slapped it against his thigh in frustration, then he jammed it back on his head as the coffee arrived. He gulped it down.

"Listen, its…uh…Reggie, right?" Jeff asked the man with Ducky. He nodded yes. "Reggie, you were plannin' on a long ride today weren't you?"

Reggie nodded again. "Mrs. Bridges asked me to return your

horse to you. Gave me a coin."

"Well, Reggie," Jeff said, pulling a biscuit out of his saddlebag and chomping on it. "How's about you keep that coin, but let me have Ducky and you just head out and pick up my milk cow. I left her about halfway between here and my place. She's tied to a rock. I wasn't sure how long I'd be gone, you see. Still not sure...." Jeff's voice trailed off as he looked around for the tracks left by the Andersons' departing wagon. He found them and stared at them while he continued. "I didn't want her to be left behind for days. She'd have been in pain and then lost her milk, but I walked her so long last night I think that ship might have sailed. Guess I wasn't thinkin' straight."

"Well, sure, sir," Reggie said. "I'll find her and I'll bring some water along for her. So, you..uh...going after your missus?"

The other men had gathered around by now and they all perked up their ears to hear Jeff's answer.

Jeff smiled, swallowing his last bite of biscuit. "I most certainly am, Reggie. I most certainly am."

A tall boy nearby grinned from ear to ear. "Well, Mr. Bridges, I'll just take this horse here to get some food and water and put her up in our barn till you get back. She looks mighty tired."

"Thank you," Jeff mumbled, as he unfastened his saddle and swung it onto Duckling's back.

"They went that way." Another man pointed to the south with a grin. "You can catch 'em. That wagon full of younguns can't go near as fast as that fresh horse of yours. Get her goin'." He clapped his hands in excitement. "Go on now!"

Jeff grinned and prodded Ducky into a gallop. He took off, following the wagon-pressed grass trail left by the Andersons. He was so close, and nothing was going to stop him from getting to Susie.

**

Riding under the autumn sun, Jeff thought of Susannah. She was all he had thought of all night long. Over the months they had spent together, Jeffrey's opinion had slowly turned from believing that a wife was an awful disturbance in a man's life to grudgingly admitting a wife might not be quite so bad. Now, he acknowledged what a fool he had been. Just as he'd been telling himself for the last few days, having a wife was more than just 'not so bad'. It was downright wonderful. It had been senseless to ignore the developing feelings forming between himself and Susie and the genuine happiness she brought to his life. His stubbornness might have cost him the best thing that ever happened to him. If he didn't get her back, his future would always feel empty, a little dimmer, a little sadder than it could have been. Having had Susannah, he could never go back to not having her. Nothing would ever be the same again. He had to find her, and stop her, and bring her back home. He had to.

Jeffrey rode south for a couple of hours and then he finally saw his wife again. He had come up over a little rise and there she was, sitting in the back of the Andersons' wagon with her legs hanging down amongst the grass. She was playing some kind of hand clapping game with one of the little girls. The child raised her hand and pointed at him and he watched as Susie's hands flew to her mouth in shock. Jeff and Duckling came trotting down from the higher ground as Susannah turned her head over her shoulder and called something out to the couple in the front. The wagon rolled to a stop just as Jeff dismounted. Susie climbed down and rushed towards him, but not as fast as he was rushing towards her.

"What's wrong?" she was saying, in an alarmed voice. "What are you doing h—"

He cut her off with a fierce hug. He wrapped his arms tight around her and squeezed her. "I found you," he said. "I found you." She could feel his heart pounding through his chest.

"Jeff.. Jeffrey... calm down." She rubbed his back like she was comforting a child.

"I had to find you, Susie," he said into her ear. "You were gone and that's what's wrong….I…I…you were gone, Susie, but you're my wife."

"It's ok," Susannah answered, still pressed against him, his nervous vice grip crushing her. "Our marriage was never what you wanted. You don't have to feel guilty about that. You don't have to feel obligated. You certainly didn't have to come all this way." She gently pushed him away, but he held her at arms' length, refusing to lose his connection to her. She kept talking in a soothing voice. "Don't worry about me. I'll be fine. Listen, I have money and I'm just going back to Seagleton, Jeff. I'll be perfectly safe there with my aunt and uncle. You won't have to wonder if I'm all right. You don't have to think about me ever again, because you'll know I'm just fine." Susannah pulled forcefully out of his grasp and stepped a short distance away. His arms hung in the air for a moment and then he dropped them. "Now," Susie said, crossing her arms in resolve, "You just ride on home, before Custard loses her milk and the chicks die. Go on now, it's ok."

She gave him a gentle shove and turned to climb back up into the wagon, but he grabbed her arm and pulled her back.

"Susie, I…," he caught his breath, "I…I can't…I can't let you go."

"Yes, you can," she said, softly. "You *can* let me go. It's ok."

A quiet moment passed as they stared at each other. The little girl tiptoed past them and took hold of Duckling's dangling reins before the horse could wander off. The couple were still staring at each other when the child walked back past them again, leading Ducky towards the front of the wagon.

Eventually, Jeff found his voice again. He looked deep into Susannah's eyes and never wanted to look away. "I…I don't want you to go, Susie. I..I want you to stay."

A hush fell over the prairie. Even the wind seemed to be stunned into silence. The grass grew still.

Ashley and her husband exchanged looks. "Um," Ashley called out, breaking the silence. She was leaning around the wagon from the front. "What say we just leave you two be for a spell. It's a good time for a break. We'll just drive on ahead a ways."

Chris flicked the reins and the wagon rolled off. Little Elinor walked along beside it with Duckling. Susie and Jeff stood staring at each other as the sounds of their friends disappeared, and the blanket of silence dropped back around them. Susie took a deep breath, listening to the return of the wandering wind sweeping across the prairie. The two of them were like specks in a sea of endless golden green. The grassland around them was slowly going to sleep for winter, its rustling brush losing color day by day. Susie felt like she was losing color too, fading away in her sorrow and confusion. She had had a plan. She didn't know what to do now. She pushed Jeffrey away again, turned and headed towards the mashed path the Anderson wagon had left.

"Susie, I'm sorry," Jeff called out, stopping her in her tracks. She did not turn around, so he spoke to her back. "I'm sorry that I didn't know what our life could be together. I'm sorry for the way I thought about women and for making you feel unwanted. No one should have to feel that way."

Susannah turned back around. "Do you think I left because I wanted an apology?" She stepped closer. "Jeff, anything you did wrong, you made up for long ago. I left because of what *I* did wrong, not you."

"What are you talking about?" he asked, his brows coming together in concern.

"You knew what you wanted and I didn't care. It was selfish, but I really believed that I could make your life better, at first." Susannah sighed. Her hands came to rest loose at her sides. "But then I started making so many mistakes that I realized I was the burden you thought I'd be."

"Are you kidding me?" Jeff responded, surprised. "I'm glad you make mistakes. It makes me feel less awful when I make them. We're just human, Susannah." He took another step closer to her. "A lost horse, making echinacea paste in the middle of the night, a fire that became a window, an exciting sinkhole nearly swallowing you up.... someday they'll all just be stories of our early years. Someday, we'll laugh at it all."

Susannah shook her head. "I don't think I'll ever laugh at being so focused on my own dreams that I took yours away." She looked down at the ground. "I saw your lifelong dreams slip away the day of our wedding. I saw it in your eyes, and it took me too long to care about that."

"Oh, Susie, my dreams were so small then. I was so wrong that day," Jeff mumbled, "About so many things." He took a deep breath and tried to explain. "Susie, my Ma never did a lick of work in her whole life, at least not that I ever saw. She was lazy, and so were all her friends. And that wasn't all. She interfered in every decision my Pa tried to make, nagging and needling and makin' him feel that everything he thought was the wrong thing to think and he couldn't do nothin' right." Jeff put his hands on his hips, remembering. "Her friends would come over to visit and sit in a circle complainin' and grumblin' the day away. That's why I used to think that women were miserable creatures, because I didn't want a life filled with all that uselessness, meanness and ungratefulness. It didn't have anything to do with thinking that a woman wouldn't make a mistake now and then, or get herself into a bit of trouble once in while." He reached for Susannah's hand and she let him take it. "That's just life, and I'm sure that I will do my fair share of making mistakes."

She smiled. "Well, maybe I'd feel better if you made one or two."

He smiled back. "What about how I was so awful to you on that first day? What about the ridiculously careless way I nearly lost us all our money in that dinky little town that I never should have taken us to?" Susannah was grinning. "What? That's not enough?" Jeff continued. "Did I ever tell you about the time I tried to fix the roof in the back storage room of the bank and the whole ceiling caved in? Pa was madder than a wet hen, cost him two days of business, plus the money to hire someone smarter than me to repair the damage. Did I tell you how I got my Grandpa's wagon all busted up driving it over a hill with too much load in the back? Cost him a pretty penny." He rubbed the back of Susannah's hand with his thumb. "I could go on."

"All right, all right," Susannah said. "I get it."

"No, you don't," Jeff stated emphatically. "I don't care about mistakes and accidents. You're not a burden, Susannah. You're a blessing. You are *not* in my way. You make my way better, and I'm just sorry that I never knew a wife could be like that."

The world grew quiet again. Susannah did not know how to respond. Tears were filling her eyes. She blinked and stared down at their intertwined hands.

Jeffrey couldn't stand the waiting. Susannah wasn't saying anything, so he kept talking.

"The truth is, I....well,....I never realized what it would be like to actually be needed." Jeff's voice came out in a whisper. "That's something I never had before and it turns out I love it." His voice grew stronger and he put his free hand under her chin and gently tilted her face up to look at him. "I really love that someone needs me. That someone is there waiting for me, wanting me, listening to me, and needing my help sometimes. I don't know how to explain it, but I don't even mind that I need you too."

"You do?" Susannah blinked, tears streaming down her face.

"I do, Susie. It just took me too long to see that." He dropped his hand from her chin and put it on her shoulder. "And I also thought that I wouldn't like always having to think about you and how things will affect you, but slowly I started to notice that

I kind of liked sharing everything with you." He sighed. "And you're always thinking of me too, going out of your way to make my life better and," he paused, "Well, I never expected how nice that would be. I thought marriage meant that I'd just be giving so much that I didn't want to give, and not getting anything back, but I was wrong." Knowing now that he couldn't live without her, Jeff let go of her hand, leaned forward and took her face into his palms. "Susannah, I love you. Please, stay with me."

Susannah felt a shiver of joy run up her spine. Her skin was growing warm and much happier tears were rushing to the surface. "But...but you wanted to be alone."

"No." Jeff shook his head. "I don't want to be alone. Not ever again."

"Ok, Jeff," she whispered, staring into his eyes. "Ok, I'll stay. I'll stay with you forever."

Relief and pure bliss washed over him. He bent and picked her up, twirling her round and round.

"Let's go home, Jeff. I love our home." She put her hand on his cheek. "You've given me everything I ever wanted."

Jeff was feeling bold. "Really?" he teased. "Well, you haven't given me everything I ever wanted." She looked at him sharply and he was quick to clarify. "I want children, Susannah. I want children with you." He smiled, thinking of the future. "I want a bunch of little girls who will turn into women just like you, and I want a son that we can teach to be better than me."

She smiled, ready to tease him back. "Well, I don't think we can have children, Jeff," she said, lightly, "Because you've never even so much as kissed me."

Jeff chuckled. "That's because I knew if I did, I'd lose my whole argument about a wife being a bad thing."

"Well, if you want a bunch of kids, you might have to get used to losing arguments."

He turned to her. "I think I'm ready for that."

She leaned towards him. "And the problem of never having kissed me?"

He smiled, reaching for her. "We can solve that problem right now."

Before she realized it was happening, Jeffrey was wrapping his arms around her. His lips met hers in a long slow kiss that made her insides flutter and her knees grow weak.

She broke free to breathe and nestled herself against his chest, feeling happier than she ever thought possible. After a moment, Jeff took her hand in his and they started walking towards the wagon. He had won her heart. She would never leave him again.

***

A day and a half later, Susie, Jeff, and their cow and horses, were back at the top of their favorite hill, gazing down at their land. It had been a long journey to get here, in more ways than one.

"Our ranch," Jeff said, waving his arm across the expanse in front of them, taking in the exquisite autumn countryside with their little farmyard snuggled into it, fitting in perfectly with the changing trees, the dying grasses and the sloping sandhills.

"Our ranch," Susie repeated, remembering how long she had wanted him to say those words. "I like the sound of that."

They dismounted, and Jeff took his wife's hand and led her down onto their ranch and back to the home they both loved. The dry golden-brown grasses slipped softly past their legs as they walked towards the cabin they had built together. They both had new dreams now. Dreams of many more things they would build together.

THE END

Dear reader, before you go.....

First of all, thank you so much for choosing to read this book. You could have picked any book, but you chose this one and I'm extremely grateful.

What did you think of <u>Arranged</u>?

I'd love to hear your honest opinion. Reviews help readers find the right book for their needs.

Feel free to share this book with your friends and family by posting about it on **Facebook** or **Twitter**.

If you enjoyed this book, I hope that you can take a quick minute to post a review on Amazon. Your feedback and support will help this author improve her craft for future projects.

I want you to know that your review is very important, so if you'd like to leave one, IT'S EASY. Just type "Arranged" into the Amazon search box, click on the book and scroll down to where it says "Write A Customer Review" on the left. **It takes less than a minute.**

Thank you for your support and I wish you happy reading in your future.

Sincerely,
Lynna Farlight

Follow me on Amazon:
amazon.com/author/lynnafarlight
Follow my blog:
https://congiles.wordpress.com/

TWO MORE BOOKS IN THIS SERIES.....

The Choiceless Marriage
Suddenly Married Book 1
By: Lynna Farlight

Mary Bingham had failed her father many times. When she burned their house down and seriously injured her littlest sister, she knew she could never make up for it, but she never imagined that her Pa would go so far as to force her to marry a stranger.

Nathaniel Hanson had been drawn to Mary since the first time he laid eyes on her. For two years she had been his dream girl, but he shouldn't have let that attraction blind him. Agreeing to marry her against her will was a mistake, and he could not undo it. All he had ever wanted was her love and now he might never have it.

Can Mary and Nathaniel somehow find their way? Together? Or will Nathaniel's mistake, and the secret darkness of Mary's past, destroy them both?

Married In The Mountains
Suddenly Married Book 2
By: Lynna Farlight

Lyssa Mayfield's dreams were crushed with the loss of her beloved husband. Now, the city girl finds herself stranded, destitute and facing a harsh winter in a dying miner's town in rough Colorado Territory. How will she ever make ends meet when she's lost in a part of the country that is unfamiliar and frightening?

A stranger wants a wife and doesn't have much time to wait for Lyssa's decision—a decision that will change her life forever and could be an irrevocable mistake. She can't imagine ever loving again, but with no home, no money, and a small child to provide for, hard choices must be made.

Dale Hawthorne is terrified of marriage and fatherhood, but he can't stand to spend another winter alone. How will he ever help this sorrowful widow find happiness again when he's never known how to find it for himself, and how will he keep her tiny daughter safe in the perilous rocky mountain homestead he's taking them to?

Can two complete strangers find their way to some kind of peaceful relationship, snowed in together in the icy mountains? Lyssa wants safety and Dale wants companionship. Will they ever have more than that, or will they come to regret their impulsive choice?

Suitable For All Audiences

Available on Amazon

Want to read another book by this author?

Nobility
By: Lynna Farlight

In the middle ages, a time of fiefdoms, where the strong rule mercilessly over the weak, one young noble dares to be different than his cruel father and one courageous young woman chooses love and selflessness over safety.

The Eltons, a family of surfs, have built a lifelong bond with the evil Duke Von Hartley's kindhearted son. Alden Von Hartley hates his father's legacy and loves the peasant Hilleena Elton, to whom he is secretly betrothed. When the couple decide to escape the misery of the fief they've grown up in and attempt to find a new home where they can live free, their plans go horribly awry. Someone dear to them is put in terrible danger and a young stranger crosses their path with a plight too dark and devastating to be ignored. Should they abandon those who need their help or risk everything to save them?

Along the way, the two brave youths fall into perilous adventures. They face injuries, starvation and the deadly pursuit of their enemy deep in the sweeping wilderness, but worst of all, Alden and Hilleena must bear being separated from each other. The decisions they make weigh heavily upon them. Will they ever find one another again and escape the clutches of those wicked men who will stop at nothing to hunt them down?

Escape into the medieval wilderness with Alden, Annora, Hilleena and Catraine as they desperately try to survive the darkness that surrounds them in a time when liberty was only a dream.

Suitable For All Audiences

Available on Amazon

Made in the USA
Monee, IL
17 March 2023

30099027R00095